Worzel Gummidge
Down Under

KEITH WATERHOUSE AND WILLIS HALL

Worzel Gummidge Down Under

DRAGON

Dragon
An imprint of the Children's
Division of the Collins Publishing Group
8 Grafton Street, London W1X 3LA

Published by Dragon Books 1987

British Library Cataloguing in Publication Data
Waterhouse, Keith
    Worzel Gummidge down under.
    I. Title   II. Hall, Willis
    823'.914[J]   PZ7

ISBN 0 583 31106 7

Printed and bound in Great Britain by Collins, Glasgow

Set in Times

Contents

Introduction

It was bright summer in England, and the hedges were heavy with blossom. As the Crowman slowly pedalled his ancient tricycle along the lane towards Ten-acre Field he hummed a quiet tune to himself and enjoyed the rich scents of hawthorn and lime. It was good to be alive! he decided. Good to be alive, and in England, and to be a Crowman going about his work.

The tricycle creaked to a halt at the gate to Ten-acre Field; the Crowman dismounted, moved to his rickety old trailer, and pulled out a bundle of straw tied up with twine. 'It's high time I gave your stomach some fresh stuffing, Worzel Gummidge,' he murmured to himself. 'It's been as messy as a pig's breakfast since that little robin nested there all spring.' He opened the gate, took one pace into the field, and stopped dead. There, in the middle of the field, was the scarecrow pole where Worzel Gummidge should have been, but instead of the scarecrow there was only a solitary rook, using one arm of the pole as a perch.

The Crowman sighed, and shook his greying head. 'Oh, Worzel, Worzel, what are you up to now?' he wondered. 'One fine summer's day, and off you go, leaving the field to the rooks.' He turned, tossed the straw back into the trailer, and clambered aboard his tricycle. 'And where shall I find you, I wonder? Scrumping green apples in old Farmer Braithwaite's orchard? Or tickling the trout at Foggy Bottom? You are a trial to me, Worzel Gummidge, and no mistake. A trial and a vexation.' But the fine day had put him in a sunny mood, and there was a smile on his weatherbeaten face as he pedalled slowly away.

The scarecrow was nowhere to be found. In the orchard the apples ripened untouched, and the trout gulped mayfly from the surface of the sluggish stream in peace. The Crowman watched them thoughtfully for a while, and slowly nodded to himself. 'Well, my fine, feckless scarecrow,' he decided, 'there's only one place left, and I can't imagine why I didn't think of it before. On such a day as this, if you're not hanging round the antique shop, trying to catch a glimpse of Aunt Sally, I'll boil my boots and eat them buttered!'

'Aunt Sally?' answered Mister Peters in surprise as the Crowman enquired after his most valuable antique. 'Why, bless you, Mister Crowman, she's been gone, oh, a month since! But if I'd known you were interested in buying her –'

'Ah, not so much interested in buying her, Mister Peters, as in ascertaining her present whereabouts,' the Crowman answered cautiously.

'Oh, well, that's easily told!' The plump little antique dealer rummaged through the litter of papers on his desk, uncovered a thick ledger, and riffled through the pages. 'I sold her ... Let's see, yes, a good month back, to a Professor Hagerty, it was, a New Zealand gentleman. Runs a Folk Museum or some such, at a village called – Here, you read it. Blessed if I can!'

The Crowman squinted at the ledger. 'Professor Hagerty,' he read slowly, 'The Folk Museum, Waiakikamokau, North Island, New Zealand.' He handed the heavy volume back and smiled. 'I'm very grateful to you for that information, Mister Peters.'

'Strange how there's so much interest in my Aunt Sally as soon as she's gone,' the shopkeeper mused.

The Crowman frowned. 'In what way?'

'Well, you're the second gentleman's been round asking after her. I say gentleman, but the other was more of a tramp, really. Scruffy-looking type, if you know what I mean. If he'd been stood in the middle of a field I could've taken him for one of your scarecrows, I reckon!'

8

The Crowman returned home grim-faced, and summoned Soggy Boggart to him. 'You were always Worzel Gummidge's closest companion,' he growled, 'and if any scarecrow knows where he's gone, it will be you.' The bedraggled figure shuffled nervously. 'Now! I charge you to tell me what you know! On pain of being thrown on to the compost heap!'

The scarecrow wriggled. ''E tol' me not to say nowt, Your Angriness,' explained Soggy Boggart. 'On account of if I did 'e'd chuck me on the bon-bon-bon-'

'And I shall most certainly chuck you on the bonfire if you do not!' promised the Crowman. 'Now for the last time, where is Worzel Gummidge?'

''E's gone, Your Mercifulness –'

'Gone? Gone where?'

'After that there Aunt Sally –'

'But where to?'

'On a hairyplane –'

'Where has Worzel Gummidge gone to!'

'To Zoo Nealand!' Soggy Boggart babbled, taking to his heels.

The Crowman waited patiently until the long shadows of dusk darkened his windows, and then reached for the telephone. 'Dusk here, dawn in New Zealand,' he murmured, dialling a long number. 'My brother should be awake by now...'

'Lines to New Zealand are engaged,' said a tinny voice in his ear. 'Please try again later.'

'Wretched invention,' he grumbled, replacing the receiver and unwrapping his crystal ball. 'The old methods always were more reliable.' The mists of time and space swirled in the little globe, and cleared at his command to reveal, on the other side of the world, his colleague, the Crowman of the Southern Cross. They exchanged formal greetings, and the Crowman of England wasted no time telling the other all that he had learned.

9

'So you think this Worzel Gummidge is on his way here, to New Zealand, chasing after Aunt Sally?'

'I'm sure of it,' the Crowman nodded.

'Then I had better look out for him.'

'I would be glad if you would, Southern Cross.' The Crowman relaxed, and smiled. 'But I must warn you; though there is no evil in him, he is a mischievous, tiresome, exasperating creature, forever finding his way into trouble...'

CHAPTER 1

The King of the Scarecrows

The New Zealand winter softened and fled, and the Crowman of the Southern Cross kept his word, and watched. It was easy enough to find the little Folk Museum at Waiakikamokau to which Aunt Sally had been sold, and then to set the sharp-eyed New Zealand Bush Hawks to watch the roads and hedgerows all around. By spring, word had reached the Crowman of Worzel's arrival, bedraggled from his long voyage, and he soon found work for the scarecrow in the fields around the little village of Pauahatanui, and a home for him in a nearby stable, where the Crowman could keep an eye on him.

As the days grew longer, the Crowman was slightly annoyed by the appearance of several new scarecrows, not of his own making, on neighbouring farms. They were ill-made, tatterdemalion things of which he would not have been proud, and their maker was robbing him of business.

On a fine October morning when the thick hedges teemed with chattering Fantails and Bellbirds the Crowman loaded up his ancient pick-up truck with the tools of his trade and set off as usual to seek work, bumping along narrow lanes still rutted from the winter rains. At a bend he slowed suddenly, for a cart was coming towards him, and in the narrow lane there was barely room for them to pass.

The cart was one he had never seen before. It jangled with pots and pans and all the paraphernalia of the tinker's trade, and it was pulled by a woebegone old horse which had clearly seen better days.

'Good morning to you!' called the Crowman, raising his tall hat with its single black crow feather politely as they passed,

11

but no answer came. Instead, the traveller raised his whip, cracked it viciously against the sad old horse's bony flanks, and hunched forward in his seat. The Crowman stared. The traveller was a strange, dirty figure, wrapped from head to foot in layers of filthy sacking. A sacking cape flapped loosely at his shoulders, and a sacking apron covered his legs. The hands that held the whip and reins were sacking-mittened, and a sacking balaclava encased his head. For a moment as they passed, his gaze turned towards the Crowman, but there was no greeting on his face; only a fixed, blind, sinister smile.

In his rear-view mirror the Crowman watched him go. 'Rednem Elttek,' he read on the tailboard of the cart. 'Rednirg Efink, Rehctaht, Rekam Llod.' There was more lettering, but before the Crowman had time to decipher it the traveller was out of sight around a bend in the road.

For a moment the Crowman sat in silence. There had been something familiar about the ugly little figure, something that struck a distant memory, and what he half-remembered made him uneasy. A village clock struck twelve, breaking into his thoughts. He shook his head and drove on.

The sound of the striking clock also reached the scarecrow. 'One bong ... three bongs ... eleventy-six bongs,' muttered Worzel Gummidge. 'Tha's a lot of bongs. In fac', so many bongs it must be knockin'-off time. Right you are, Worzel, that's enough rooks scared for one day!' He clambered down from his scarecrow-pole, flexed his twiggy limbs and gazed happily round the potato-field. 'It's all yours, you rooks,' he announced. 'Back termorrer ...' and he stumped away across the furrows towards a little wood, singing as he went. 'Ho, one man an' his dog, went for to mow a meadow, one man, 'alf a man an' his dog, went for to mow a meadow.'

On the far side of the same wood the Crowman halted his battered old truck and clambered out. Curious crows wheeled above and settled in the tall elms to peer down at him.

12

Humming contentedly to himself, the Crowman lovingly lifted a newly-made scarecrow, stiff and lifeless, from the back of the truck and carried it carefully into the wood to a quiet clearing beneath the arms of a great oak. With a heavy stone he hammered a pole into the soft earth, and then he hauled the scarecrow up into position on it. 'There you are, my beauty,' he murmured to himself, as the crows flapped ungainly down to take a closer look.

They were not the only watchers. At the Crowman's back a pair of unblinking eyes peered through a gap in a hawthorn bush, but the Crowman was intent on his work, and suspected nothing.

He stepped back, inspected his creation, and nodded in satisfaction. The work was almost complete. He looked around in the little clearing until he found an acorn-twig, and lifted it high to start the naming ceremony. 'Apples for health,' he began, 'corn for plenty, berries for happiness. By the wind and the rain and all the seasons, I name this scarecrow ...'

A horse whinnied. The Crowman broke off, lowered the twig, and swung round angrily. There was nothing to be seen in the little clearing, but the leaves of a hawthorn bush were moving, though there was no wind. His eyes narrowed as he strode forward, paused for a moment, and turned back to the scarecrow. 'On second thoughts,' he announced grimly, 'I'll name thee and give thee life when prying eyes aren't watching.' He raised his tall hat politely to the lifeless scarecrow, then turned again to push his way through the empty trees. As he neared his truck, a scrap of dirty sacking caught on a thorn met his eye and he fingered it thoughtfully.

Crows wheeled noisily overhead, breaking into his thoughts. The Crowman climbed into the driving seat and lifted his head to growl at them, 'Caw, caw, as you please! The ceremony is postponed!'

As the Crowman drove off there was a distant rumble of thunder, and he hesitated, wondering whether to turn back, but after a moment the noise died away and he drove on, reassured.

In the clearing, the scarecrow twitched. Something in the power of the thunder had reached down into the lifeless figure to finish what the Crowman's making-words had begun. There was another roll of thunder, like the drums of a distant army, and the scarecrow's arms and legs thrashed this way and that as he struggled to finish coming to life. Once more the thunder drifted away and died, and the scarecrow drooped limply back into lifelessness.

From his hiding-place behind the thick hawthorn, the ragged sacking-clad figure watched and waited...

'Ho, eleventy men went for to mow a meadow, eleventy men, six men, ninety-nine men, four men, eighteen men, three men and his dog, went for to mow...'

Worzel Gummidge was happy.

He had abandoned scaring crows for the day.

He had seen no sign of the Crowman wanting to return him to his field.

And as he stumped stiff-legged through the sleepy little village of Pauahatanui he swigged cold milk from a bottle he had taken from a doorstep. He paused, and his sharp little eyes gleamed as he spotted a freshly-baked pie cooling on a window-sill.

'My, my, my! If there's one thing nearly as good as a cup o' tea and a slice o' cake when the day's crow-scarin's done, it's a bokkle o' milk and a meat-an'-tatie pie,' Worzel chortled cheerfully. The pie had obviously been put on the window-sill for him to take, so he took it, crashing through the hedge and tramping down the flowers. 'My, my, my!' he breathed as he sniffed the pie, and found it good. He held it at arm's length in front of him so that the rich meaty smell wafted over him as he followed it out of the village.

'Ho, twelvety men went for to mow,' he sang, 'went to mow

a meadow. Twelvety men, eleventy men, six men, nine men, four men...' At the sound of the Crowman's old truck he broke off and scuttled to take cover behind a tree, carefully clutching his milk and his meat and potato pie. The wheezing sound of the familiar pick-up approached, passed, and slowly faded away. Worzel Gummidge cautiously stepped out from his hiding-place with a sigh of relief.

'Cor, that was a near one an' no mistake,' he told himself. 'Best make ee-self scarce, Worzel, in case 'is blumptitude comes back!' and without further ado he plunged into the wood, munching the pie and swilling the milk as he went. Crashing through the undergrowth he suddenly burst out into the little clearing where the Crowman had been, and his turnip features beamed with pleasure at the sight of the new scarecrow hanging there on his pole.

'My, my, my, you've doed it again, Mister Crowman,' Worzel cried, as proud as if he'd done it himself. There was a clamour of rooks above his head, and he hurled the empty milk bottle and pie-dish at them. 'There you are, you pesky rooks – if he goes on at this rate there'll be more of us nor what there is of you. *Then* you'll cop it!' He crept towards the lifeless scarecrow. 'My, you's an ugly customer an' no mistake,' he decided. 'Nearly as ugly as ol' Worzel.'

He wriggled his ungainly body into a stiff, formal pose, and wordlessly began the long series of arm-wavings and leg-wagglings, hat-doffings and coat-tailings, bowings and scrapings, that make up the secret and proper ritual greeting known to all scarecrows.

There was no response from the stranger.

Worzel frowned. 'Oy! I'm a-greeting' of 'ee!' he growled, insulted. 'Don't 'ee know your scarecrow greetin' yet?'

The force of Worzel's words awoke another part of the new scarecrow's mind, as the thunder had done before, and the Crowman before the thunder. It lurched on its pole, and spoke with difficulty in a deep, rasping voice. 'Ooooo ... Aarrrr...'

15

'Then greet me proper, else I'll kick the begubbins out of 'ee,' demanded Worzel Gummidge reasonably. He began the little ceremony again. 'Now then ... One, four, six –' He swept off his hat. The new scarecrow jerkily did the same. The scarecrow greeting had begun. It had never been meant for outside eyes, but this time, as the two performed the age-old moves, the leaves of the hawthorn bush parted again and a pair of sinister eyes stared through...

In a few more minutes the long ritual was done. The movements had loosened some of the stiffness from the new scarecrow's limbs, and eased his throat. Worzel Gummidge beamed at him. 'That's more like it. Better out nor in, the scarecrow greetin' is. Now we can be sociab... socialab... friendly like. My name's Worzel Gummidge – what's yours?'

The other thought for a moment. 'A cup o' tea an' a slice o' cake, thank 'ee, Worzel Gummidge,' he decided.

'You daft hearthbrush! I didn't mean wha's 'ee want to eat! I meant what's your name?'

The new scarecrow looked blank. 'Name?' he asked.

'Yes – name,' explained Worzel patiently. 'Like as it might be Hessian Tatersack else Soggy Boggart. What you got called when you got life brethed into you.'

'I wasn't called nothing that I knows of, Worzel Gummidge. I don't think I's got a name,' the scarecrow confessed rather apologetically.

Worzel was astonished. 'No name? I's never 'eard 'o sich a thing!' he declared. He scratched his sprouting head with twiggy fingers, amazed at the Crowman's negligence. 'That's what comes o' making' scarecrows twelvety to the dozen,' he muttered. ''E's turnin' 'em out so fast 'e's forgettin' to finish 'em off proper... Either that or 'e's goin' soft in the 'ead.'

The new scarecrow coughed apologetically to catch Worzel's attention. 'Does all other scarecrows 'ave names, Worzel Gummidge?' he asked wistfully.

16

''Course they does. Until you been given your name, you ain't been properly brung to life.'

The other looked crestfallen. 'Ain't I? Is that why I tumbles over when I tries to get off me pole?'

'It must be,' frowned Worzel. His frown deepened with effort as he had a good think. ''Ere – you's *susposed* to 'ave a name ... 'Ow's about if I gives you one, seein' as it's been overlooked?'

The new scarecrow beamed with delight, and wriggled on its pole. 'You, Worzel Gummidge?'

'Oo, ar! I might look like just another stewpid old scarecrow to you, but –' He tapped his carrot nose knowingly and gave a wink. 'I knows 'ow it's done, see. Now then, let's just find an acorn twig.'

On Worzel's words there was a hissing intake of breath from the ragged watcher behind the hawthorn, but the two scarecrows were too busy with what they were doing to hear it. Besides, there was at that moment another low, rumbling murmur of thunder, as though it were commenting on what Worzel Gummidge was doing, and a cawing from the rooks above, just as if they too understood and disapproved. Worzel Gummidge cocked an ear to the distant rumble and an eye to the sky, but failed to heed the warnings. 'Comin' on to rain, by the sound of it,' he commented cheerfully as he picked up the Crowman's discarded acorn twig. 'It's a good job all us scarecrows 'as umbrellies ... Now then, 'ow does it go?'

He raised the twig high over the other scarecrow's head as he had seen the Crowman do so often, and took a deep breath. 'Now let's 'ave a go ... Apples for health, corn for plenty, bushey ... no – berries for happiness – by the wind and er ... the rain and all the seasons, I name this scarecrow ... Now what *shall* I name this scarecrow?'

The effort was too much for him. He was thinking so hard that he snapped the twig in his own twiggy fingers, completing the ceremony. 'Dangnation take it!' he cried.

17

The skies darkened, and a terrible clap of thunder broke directly over the clearing, rousing all the rooks to a massive outburst of cawing. As the birds wheeled and croaked above his head the scarecrow began to have second thoughts about what he was doing. 'Now what's I done ...? Mebbe I shouldn't name this scarecrow after all. Mebbe I should leave it to them what knows better,' he decided, too late.

Another clap of thunder rippled angrily round the clearing and the new scarecrow wrenched himself awkwardly from his pole, swayed for a moment, and then threw himself at Worzel Gummidge's feet. 'Oh, Your Majesty!' he cried. 'Your omniepant Majesty!'

Worzel looked bemused. 'Majesty? What do you mean? Get up, you daft lummock!' he ordered.

But the new scarecrow stayed just where he was, kneeling before Worzel Gummidge, embracing his beanpole legs, and moaning with pleasure. 'Your Majesty, you have gave me a name and said the scarecrow blessing and broke the twig over my 'ead, so now I am properly alive.'

Worzel looked nervously round, as if the Crowman might somehow have overheard. 'Gave you a name?' he whispered. 'Now just 'ang on a minute, don't you go around sayin' I's give you no name!'

'But you 'as, Your Majesty,' insisted the other joyfully. '"Dangnation Take It."'

'"Dangnation Take It" ain't a name!' yelped Worzel, realizing what had happened and wondering what he was going to tell the Crowman.

'It's a wonderful name, Your Majesty!' the new scarecrow declared. 'And now I'm a proper walking, talking scarecrow. I thanks you from the bottom of my straw, O King Of The Scarecrows!'

Worzel was baffled. 'King o' the Scarecrows? Me? King o' the Scarecrows? You great soft ...' He paused for a moment as the idea began to grow on him. 'King o' the Scarecrows, eh? Whyfor do you think I's King o' the Scarecrows?'

The new scarecrow gazed up at Worzel with adoring eyes. 'You must be, Your Majesty, to 'ave magic powers.'

'That's true enough,' agreed Worzel, half to himself. 'King o' the Scarecrows, eh? Wait till I tells Aunt Sally! She'll want to marry me then!' he gurgled. 'Me King o' the Scarecrows an' 'er me Queen ... It'll make 'er the 'appiest Aunt Sally in the 'ole Scarecrow world!' He looked down at the new scarecrow, still shuffling about on his knees, and adopted a kingly manner. 'Well,' he declared, 'mebbe I is King o' the Scarecrows – Did I say you could rise?' he snapped.

'I wasn't rising, Your Majesty. I was just going to kiss your boots.'

Worzel sniffed. 'Go on then, Dangnation Take It – get 'em kissed. Then I've got one or two other little jobs wants doin' – like fetchin' the King o' the Scarecrows a cup o' tea and a slice o' cake.'

'Yes, Your Majesty ...' beamed Dangnation Take It obediently.

Worzel raised his right boot. 'Leftest one first ...'

The leaves of the hawthorn bush closed, and the ragged watcher slipped silently away...

CHAPTER 2

The Travelling Scarecrow-Maker

Across the fields, on the outskirts of the little village of Pauahatanui, was the rambling collection of barns and potting-sheds and stables around the old farmhouse where the Crowman of the Southern Cross had his home. Inside, the Crowman himself was hard at work, building another new scarecrow with all his usual care. From the courtyard outside there came the unmistakeable sounds of a horse and cart drawing up, but the Crowman gave no sign that he had heard, and worked quietly on.

The sacking-clad traveller slid down to the ground and rummaged around in the chaos of pots and pans, mangles and scythes and grinding-wheels in the cart. He selected a battered old copper kettle, and slithered across the courtyard and through the open door of the Crowman's workshop. The Crowman ignored him and went on working, so that eventually the strange figure was reduced to giving an apologetic cough.

'Yes, what do you want?' asked the Crowman coldly.

The other's manner was humble. 'Good morrow, Master.'

'I'm not your master,' replied the Crowman bluntly. 'State your business.'

The traveller grovelled, and reached under his sacking cloak. 'I've brought you a gift, Master,' he whined. 'A fine kettle.'

The Crowman turned with a sigh and stared at the traveller. 'Thank you, I have my own kettle.'

From beneath his filthy cloak, with all the speed of a magician, the traveller produced a succession of grubby and unlikely items. 'A boiling pot, then?' he suggested. 'A toasting-fork? A flat iron? A lamp? A lucky mascot? A doll?' With his last words he threw aside his cloak to reveal, pinned inside, a display of horrible, miniature scarecrow dolls.

The Crowman stepped back, upset. 'Get those things out of my sight!' he hissed.

The traveller gave a cringing bob. 'Your honour has a sharp tongue, to one whose only thought it to welcome him ... A colleague –' he added slyly.

The Crowman's eyes narrowed. 'Colleague? I'm no colleague of yours!'

'A travelling scarecrow-maker?'

'Hmph! There are scarecrows and scarecrows,' the Crowman growled.

The traveller nodded agreement. 'There are, Master, and yours are second to none. I've been looking at some of your scarecrows.' The words seemed to crawl greasily out of his thin-lipped mouth.

The Crowman stared scornfully down at him. 'And I at some of yours. You're a disgrace to your craft.'

'I'm just a poor, honest Scarecrow-maker, although very much inferior to yourself. Oh, what a talent you have in those hands, Master.'

'That's enough of that!' snapped the Crowman sharply. 'I don't need your slimy praise.'

'Would that I had a quarter of your powers, Master,' cringed the other.

There was a long silence. At length the Crowman answered. 'Powers? You have your own powers,' he growled knowingly.

The traveller shook his grey head. 'None, Master. I have no powers.'

'I know very well what you have and how you use them!' The Crowman's dark eyes flashed fire as he spoke, and there was a terrible strength in his quiet voice. 'As for mine, they are

21

nothing compared with those of the Crowman of all Crowmen.'

'But I know that they are, Master,' the traveller insisted. 'I have seen them.'

'Seen them?' There was a note of worry in the Crowman's voice.

'Scarecrows. Walking and talking – by daylight.'

'Poppycock! Where do you claim to have seen my scarecrows walking and talking?'

The traveller looked triumphant. 'In Long Meadow, Master – and not very long ago ... walking ... talking ... and speaking the language your honour puts into their turnip heads.'

The Crowman groaned, and muttered to himself. 'Worzel Gummidge!'

'Worzel Gummidge? Is that a scarecrow's name, Master?'

'Mind your own business.'

'Worzel Gummidge. That's a fine name for a scarecrow, Master. I'll remember Worzel Gummidge.'

The Crowman pointed a long, bony finger at the traveller and spoke sternly, making the other fall back in alarm. 'You leave my scarecrows alone, do you hear?'

'But I don't want your scarecrows, Master,' he insisted. 'Only your secret.'

The Crowman grew calm again, like a thunderstorm folding back upon itself. There was even the hint of a wry smile on his face as he replied. 'The only secret I possess is one you could never learn.'

With desperation in his voice the traveller produced from his cloak a heavy money bag and threw a handful of coins into the air. 'A crock of gold for your secret, Master!'

'Keep your gold,' laughed the Crowman. He snapped his fingers, and the falling shower of gold became no more than dust in the bright sunlight, and vanished before it hit the ground.

The traveller looked sly, and tried one final offer. 'A lucky mascot for your secret,' he said slowly. From the depths of his sacking costume he produced one of his ugly miniature scarecrows and held it out to the Crowman. Its head seemed to glitter and shimmer in the bright light.

'No! No!' As the Crowman backed away in alarm the traveller advanced towards him, the horrible doll held high, his voice silky and low.

'Your secret, Master, that's all I ask for ... Just the secret of your powers ... Take the lucky mascot, Master,' he pleaded. 'Take the talisman.'

The Crowman pulled himself up to his full height and snatched down a sickle from the wall. '*That* for your talisman!' he roared, and with a sweep of the weapon knocked the ugly, mis-shapen doll into the fire. The flames caught it instantly, and in a sudden burst of acrid black smoke it was gone, and all its dark power with it. The Crowman advanced on the traveller, who began to slither away in fear. 'And now, my friend,' he declared grimly, 'I think I've had enough of you!' Still bobbing cringingly, the traveller scuttled out of the workshop and into the courtyard, and clambered hurriedly on to his cart. 'Now, clear off ... and don't come back!' shouted the Crowman.

The traveller touched his forelock politely. 'We'll meet again, Master. Oh yes, we'll meet again. And I'll be sure to remember your Honour's favourite scarecrow ... Worzel Gummidge.'

As he watched him go, the Crowman shook his head and sighed, puzzled. 'Cringing to the last,' he mused. 'Still calling me Master ... as though I had some power over him. These are strange times, very strange...'

In a disused stable on the outskirts of Pauahatanui the King of the Scarecrows was enthroned in splendour on a rickety pile of old orange boxes. Round his scrawny shoulders was a moth-eaten eiderdown rescued from a rubbish dump which served as

23

his cloak, and his crown was a battered old toffee-tin perched at a jaunty angle. He made a rather messy job of gnawing a chicken leg, tossed it over his shoulder, and smacked his lips with relish. He gazed around his palace in satisfaction, and his eye fell on the dog-eared photograph of his maker, the Crowman of all Crowmen, which he had cherished throughout his travels and pinned on the stable wall.

'Oo, you don't 'alf look vexed, Mister proper Crowman, sir – it's a good job you ain't 'ere,' Worzel admitted to himself. ''Cos if you was you'd 'ave Worzel's 'ead in a stewpot with carrots an' dumplin's for what I's doin'. Well, I'll tell 'ee what, your absenteeship, I'll only be King o' The Scarecrows jus' for a bit, and then I'll go back to being plain ol' Worzel again, so don't you go blabbing to the Zoo Nealand Crowman, will yer?' Having thus made his peace with his maker Worzel reached out for a rusty old handbell and rang it loudly. Dangnation Take It shuffled into the stable and threw himself at Worzel's feet. The King sniffed. 'What took you so long?' he demanded.

'A thousand pardings, O King o' the Scarecrows,' wailed his courtier. 'I'll come quicker next time.'

'You'd better, else I'll 'ave your 'ead for piccalilli.' Worzel looked down at the grovelling figure and planted a hefty boot on the back of its head, squashing its face down into the dust.

'What is your Majesty's pleasure?' asked Dangnation Take It with some difficulty through a mouthful of straw and dirt.

The King Of The Scarecrows' pleasures didn't change much. 'A cup o' tea an' a slice o' cake – that's my pleasure. So get it fetched and be quick about it.'

Dangnation Take It hesitated. 'But may it please your Majesty, your Majesty's already 'ad eleventy cups o' tea an' slices o' cake this afternoon,' he pointed out.

Worzel Gummidge pressed Dangnation Take It's head down again with his boot. 'An' I shall 'ave plenty more if I wants! I shall 'ave as many cups o' tea an' slices o' cake as you can lay your twiggy 'ands on! What's the sense in bein' King o'

24

the Scarecrows if a body can't have all the cups o' tea an' slices o' cake 'e wants?' he pointed out reasonably.

Dangnation Take It couldn't argue with that. 'Yes, Your Majesty ... Straight away Your Majesty!' he agreed, rescuing his head and backing away towards the door on all fours.

"Ere – an' don't forget!' called Worzel as he left. 'Keep a sharp eye open for my Aunt Sally. An' if you see 'er, tell 'er if she wants to be Queen o' the Scarecrows she'd better get down 'ere as fast as 'er wooden legs'll carry 'er!'

'Yes, your Omnicopence!' cried the scarecrow, and fled.

Worzel looked about him, licking his lips. 'It's 'ungry work bein' King o' the Scarecrows. Now where did I chuck that chicken bone?' and he clambered down from his throne to scrabble around in the dirt and straw.

'Mildew Turnip! Stop! What are you doing here?' The Crowman's words rang out loud and clear in the quiet street on the fringes of Pauahatanui. Dangnation Take It, carrying on his head an upturned dustbin lid piled high with cream cakes he had just taken from an unattended baker's van, looked puzzled. 'Doing here ...' he echoed. 'Me ...? Eh? Get out of my way!'

'How dare you say that to me!' exploded the Crowman. 'Don't you know who I am?'

The scarecrow looked him up and down. 'No – I don't know who you is!' he retorted.

'Hasn't Worzel Gummidge told you? Don't lie to me – I know you've been talking to Worzel! You were seen!'

A great, happy, beaming smile broke out on the scarecrow's face. 'Oh, I know 'oo you must be now – Aunt Sally.'

The Crowman turned beetroot red. 'Mildew Turnip! Do I look like Aunt Sally?'

"Ow do I know if I've never seen 'er?' answered Dangnation Take It logically. 'An' why do you keep calling me Mildew Turnip?'

'Because, Mildew Turnip, Mildew Turnip happens to be your name.'

'No it ain't.'

'Yes it is.'

'No it ain't.'

'Yes it is.'

'No it ain't.'

The Crowman was furious. He was not used to such blatant disobedience, even from Worzel Gummidge. 'How dare you contradict ...?' He stopped. Suddenly he remembered the events of the morning, and with a great effort calmed himself down. 'I do apologize, Mildew Turnip. I beg your pardon. I've just remembered – the naming ceremony was not completed. But you may take it from me – your name is definitely Mildew Turnip.'

'And *you* can take it from *me*,' replied Dangnation Take It firmly, 'that my name is Dangnation Take it.'

The Crowman looked bemused. '"Dangnation Take It"?' he echoed. 'What kind of a name is that?'

Dangnation Take It's chest swelled with pride as he answered. 'It's the name what was give to me – by 'is Royal Majesty King Worzel the First, King o' the Scarecrows.'

'King of the ...!' squawked the Crowman. 'What *are* you talking about ...? No ... I don't believe it! Not even Worzel!'

'King Worzel, if you please,' insisted Dangnation Take It. 'And now, if you'll hexcuse me, 'is Majesty hawaits.'

The Crowman nodded, and let him pass. 'Yes, I'll excuse you, for you act in ignorance. Off you go ... But Worzel! You I can't forgive.'

A thunderous hammering on the old stable door awoke the King Of The Scarecrows from a doze on his throne.

'Henter!' he bellowed regally.

Dangnation Take It entered. 'May it please Your Majesty,' he bawled, 'Your Majesty's grub!'

Worzel Gummidge rubbed his palms together and licked his lips in anticipation. 'Hadvance, my Majesty's Grub, an' be etten!' he commanded, and Dangnation Take It made his way with all the dignity of a butler across the dingy stable, his dustbin lid of cakes held aloft. The King Of The Scarecrows examined them greedily. 'Oo, eleventy-twelve jam tarts! I 'aven't 'ad a jam tart since 'alf an hour ago. But where's me cup o' tea, you idle lummock?'

The courtier looked suitably apologetic. 'I couldn't get you no tea, O King, so I got you a tin o' limmonade.'

'Limmonade, eh?' Worzel Gummidge's beady eyes lit up. 'Ar, well, lucky for you, I likes limmonade. So you can grovel while I drinks it.'

'Your wish is my command, O King!' cried Dangnation Take It happily, throwing himself headlong into the straw at his King's feet. Neither he nor Worzel Gummidge, intent on his food, noticed the stable door swing quietly open and a dark figure slip into the shadows.

Worzel Gummidge examined the can of lemonade suspiciously, as though he had never seen one before – which, indeed, he hadn't. He held it to his carrot nose and sniffed it, then to his ear and listened to it, then gave it a thoroughly good shake and tried his teeth on it. 'Dang-blasted thing, why won't it open!' he growled grumpily.

'Can I offer my 'umble assistance, O King o' the Scare–' began Dangnation Take It, lifting his head. He caught sight of the dark figure and got his head down again. 'Oo-er!' he finished.

'What you mean "Oo-er?" 'Ow will an "Oo-er" get this tin-can open?' asked Worzel, poking at the ring-pull. Dangnation Take It kept his head down and raised a twiggy thumb to point over his shoulder at the advancing figure.

Worzel looked where he pointed.

He gawped.

It was at that moment that he discovered how to open a ring-

27

pull can, and drenched the Crowman in a torrent of sticky, fizzy lemonade. 'Aaaaaargh,' Worzel gasped, paralysed. 'It's … what's … 'cos … 'ow … 'oo –'

Dangnation Take It bravely lifted his head. 'It's all right, O King! It's only an 'armless yewman what's daft in the 'ead …'

Worzel gibbered with fright. ''E … ah … ah … 'e … Take no notice of 'im, yore effluence … 'E's even dafter than what you is, which you ain't. 'E don't mean you're 'armless … It's just 'e don't know no –'

'Silence!!!!' roared the Crowman.

The King Of The Scarecrows went on gibbering until he ran out of steam. 'Yes … yes, your 'oliness … your reverence … your …' As a last desperate remedy he held out the dustbin lid full of cakes. 'Would you like a jam tart, Your Majesty?' he wheedled.

With a sweep of his arm the angry Crowman sent the lid and the cakes flying across the stable. The ex-King Of The Scarecrows glanced miserably at the photograph of his maker. 'Oo … er … 'E's worse nor what you is when 'e gets 'is dander up, your angriness.'

Dangnation Take It was annoyed to see all his carefully-stolen food go flying, and looked up from under his brows at his King. ''Ere!' he announced angrily, rising to his feet. 'Now they's got straw all on 'em. Shall I pull 'is 'at over 'is eyes, O King?'

'Worzel,' said the Crowman in a voice full of menace. 'I think you'd better tell Mildew Turnip who I am.'

Dangnation Take It was fed up. ''E keeps calling me that, O King, but I tell 'im my name's Dangnation Take It.'

Worzel Gummidge shook his head miserably. 'Your name ain't Dangnation Take It, Dangnation Take It. If Mister Crowman sez so, it's Mildew Turnip.'

'Mister Crowman?' whispered Mildew Turnip.

Worzel Gummidge nodded at him. 'Your maker – Your maker what brethed life into you.'

Mildew Turnip hit the floor again and pressed himself into the straw. 'Mister Crowman – I never – I didn't know,' he wailed.

'I know you didn't, Mildew Turnip.' For the ignorant scarecrow his voice was gentle and forgiving. 'Get on your feet.'

Mildew Turnip stayed down and, in a voice muffled with straw, explained, 'I'd rather kneel an' grovel for a bit to be on the safe side, if it's all the same to you, O Mister Crowman ... 'Cos if you're Mister Crowman, O Mister Crowman, that means you must be even 'igher and mightier than 'is Majesty the King o' the Scarecrows 'ere.'

Worzel cringed where he sat, and tried to hide his toffee-tin crown. 'Sssh! I ain't the King o' the Scarecrows, Mildew Turnip. Just an 'umble 'ank o' straw with a turnip 'ead, same as you.'

The Crowman drew himself up to his full height and said sternly, 'It makes no difference, Worzel Gummidge. You meddled in matters you do not comprehend. You interfered in the sacred process of scarecrow-making. You uttered the scarecrow blessing and filled Mildew Turnip's head with seditious nonsense. I am the Crowman of the Southern Cross, Worzel Gummidge. My authority will not be usurped by my own creations. I cannot allow it. Do you understand what I'm saying to you?'

'Yes, Mister Crowman, sir.'

'You know the penalty?'

'Yes, Mister Crowman, sir.'

'There can be no appeal.'

The pathetic scarecrow's watery eye fell on the tatty photograph. 'Not even to Mister Crowman, Mister Crowman, sir?' he tried.

'To nobody. You will follow me now to my house, Worzel Hedgerow Gummidge, where you will be given your last supper.'

The response was automatic. 'A cup o' tea an' a slice o' cake, Mister Crowman sir?'

'If that is your wish. Sentence will be carried out at midnight. Come along.'

'Yes, Mister Crowman, sir.'

The Crowman led a sorry procession out of the stable and across the fields, his expression stern. A doleful Worzel followed, head hung low, and Mildew Turnip brought up the rear, nervous and bewildered. None of them noticed the travelling scarecrow-maker, his grey sacking clothes making him all but invisible in the twilight, watching with interest from the edge of the wood.

It was nearly midnight.

In the little cobbled courtyard outside the Crowman's workshop a huge bonfire had been built of dry old branches, discarded packing cases and bundles of newspapers done up with string. All the birds and animals seemed to have left the place deserted, and only the travelling scarecrow-maker was there to witness what was to happen, lurking behind a low hedge on the far side of the lane.

Indoors, Worzel Gummidge was sitting miserably at the Crowman's laden tea-table, a great pot of tea and a huge chocolate cake in front of him. The tea was growing cold, untouched. Only one slice had been cut from the cake, and that lay forlorn on the scarecrow's plate, a single mouse-sized bite nibbled out of it. There was a crackling from the courtyard, and through the window Worzel could see flickering flames rising. The Crowman came in, grim-faced, and looked around. 'You haven't made a very good job of your last supper, Worzel.'

He nodded glum agreement. 'I knows, Mister Crowman, sir ... It's the firstest time I 'aven't 'et up every crumb of a slice o' cake ... an I expects it'll be the lastest.'

A distant clock began to chime, and the Crowman compared it with his huge pocket watch. 'It's time, Worzel. Stand.' The scarecrow rose shuffling to his feet. 'Any last words?'

'Will you give this slice o' cake to my Aunt Sally, your Worship, an' look after er?'

'I'll keep an eye on her, Worzel,' he promised. The clock finished striking. 'Midnight. Follow me.' He led the way solemnly out of the house and into the courtyard, Worzel Gummidge shuffling miserably along behind. Suddenly the Crowman stopped, the scarecrow almost bumping into him, and peered keenly into the shadows. 'Wait!' he hissed. 'I see you there, fellow!' he called loudly. 'Come out and state your business!'

Out of the shadows crept the travelling scarecrow-maker, little more than a shadow himself, wringing his hands beside the flickering bonfire. 'Good evening, Master,' he said greasily. 'What an honour to be in your Honour's household ... And this must be Master Gummidge.'

The scarecrow was past caring. ''Ow-de-do, sir,' he called cheerily. 'Any friend o' Mister Crowman's is a friend o' mine, sir.'

The Crowman's quiet words to Worzel were heavy with warning. 'He's no friend, Worzel.' He stared at the travelling scarecrow-maker. 'What do you want?'

'To pay my respects, Master ... And to give Master Gummidge a present.'

'Very kind of 'ee, sir,' said the scarecrow politely. 'But a prezzie's no use to me where I's goin'. Ain't that right, Mister Crowman?'

'This one might be. It will help you, Master Gummidge ... Take it,' the traveller hissed urgently, plunging a mittened hand into the depths of his sacking cloak and drawing out one of his horrible miniature scarecrow dolls. Its tiny, ugly head was shimmering and sparkling with light, and Worzel Gummidge gazed open-mouthed at it.

31

'In that case, sir, thank 'ee very much ... Oh, it's a titchy little scarec...'

'Don't touch it!' The Crowman's words crackled like flames through the night as Worzel reached out to take the doll.

Worzel shrugged apologetically at the travelling scarecrow-maker. 'Sorry, sir. I allus does what Mister Crowman tells me,' he explained.

The Crowman raised his eyes to the night sky at the scarecrow's words. 'Oh, Worzel, I wish you had,' he sighed, half to himself. 'This creature is the Travelling Scarecrow-Maker, and I know now why he's here.'

Worzel scratched his turnip head. 'Travellin' Scarecrow-Maker? What ...? Another Crowman, Mister Crowman, sir? There's more o' you nor crows!'

'But without his Honour's powers, Master Gummidge,' crawled the travelling scarecrow-maker.

Very quietly, so that the scarecrow scarcely noticed, the Crowman moved away from the fire and into the shadows, leaving Worzel Gummidge and the travelling scarecrow-maker face to face. His words came softly out of the darkness. 'Don't believe him. He has powers, black powers.'

'I have none,' the other insisted.

Worzel was fascinated. 'Can 'e breth scarecrows to life like what you can, Mister Crowman?'

'After his fashion.' The grim voice became suddenly sharp, and the travelling scarecrow-maker jumped at the Crowman's words. 'Let your acolytes come forward!'

'They're poor things, Master,' the traveller grovelled. 'Only poor things, not worth your Honour's attention.'

The Crowman strode out of the darkness, towering over the cowering figure. He grabbed the travelling scarecrow-maker's arm and thrust it high in the air, so that the little talisman that he was still clutching glittered and glimmered above their heads. 'Let them come forward, I say!' he ordered.

The travelling scarecrow-maker wrenched himself free. 'As

your Honour commands,' he spat. From his thin lips there came a sound somewhere between a hiss and a whistle, and Worzel gawped in astonishment as out of the shadows lumbered two tall, terrible figures. At first they appeared to be scarecrows like himself, but as they drew closer to the fire he saw that they were ill-made, ugly creatures. Their walk was cumbersome and lumbering, and their faces were blank and expressionless. They took up their positions on either side of their maker.

'Hey ... What's them?' he gasped. 'Them things ... They's ... They's alive – yet they's not alive!'

The Crowman nodded, grim-faced in the flickering firelight. 'Correct, Worzel. They cannot talk, they have no thoughts, they do not sing, or dance, or smile. They walk only when a talisman is placed in their hands – and then they walk only by night. At cockcrow, they become scarecrows again. They exist only to carry out this creature's bidding. They are his scarecrow-slaves,' he finished, moving silently aside again to stand in the shadows.

The travelling scarecrow-maker seemed almost proud of what the Crowman was saying about him. 'Poor things, Master ... But my own,' he boasted.

Worzel frowned, and scratched his head. 'What is it they does, when they walks by night, Mister Crowman, sir?'

'Evil, Worzel. Evil, bad things.' The Crowman's words came softly out of the darkness. He turned to the travelling scarecrow-maker and gestured towards the confused scarecrow. 'Now, Traveller, tell Worzel Gummidge what you want of him.'

Worzel Gummidge gawped. 'Of me, sir? Poor ol' Worzel what's bout to be throwed on the bon- on the bon- on the bon-' he hiccupped.

'Not necessarily, Master Gummidge,' the travelling scarecrow-maker hissed.

'What's he mean, Mister Crowman sir, not necessess...'

The Crowman's reply was sombre. 'Pay attention to him, Worzel...'

The travelling scarecrow-maker put his blank face close to Worzel's. 'I have other scarecrows, Master Gummidge, besides these two,' he whispered persuasively. 'They are surrounding his Honour's house. You do not have to be put to the flames.'

'Why for not? What does I 'ave to do?'

'Come with me, Master Gummidge. I can save you. Take this and come with me!' and he thrust forward the ugly little talisman, shimmering now more brightly than ever.

'Do you 'ear that, Mister Crowman, sir? 'E sez to go with 'im!'

'I hear him, Worzel.'

Worzel was baffled. Moments before he had been doomed to the flames for disobedience, and now he was seemingly being offered the chance to escape. 'Well ain't you goin' to stop me?' he demanded.

'No, Worzel, you're free to go.'

The travelling scarecrow-maker pushed the talisman close to the scarecrow's face. 'Come, Master Gummidge. Take it ... Take it ...' he hissed, as his two expressionless slaves beckoned Worzel Gummidge with uncoordinated arms, like windmills in a slow wind.

Worzel stepped forward, then hesitated as a thought struck him. ''Ere!' he demanded indignantly. 'If I *does* take it, will I be like them?'

'You'll be saved from the flames, Master Gummidge.'

'Only comin' alive at night, an' not talkin' nor thinkin' nor singin' nor smilin' ... Nor lovin' my Aunt Sally?'

'Saved from the flames!' There was a desperate urgency in the travelling scarecrow-maker's voice that was obvious even to Worzel.

'Your scarecrow slave?' he asked, then half-turned to the Crowman.

The Crowman shook his head. 'The decision is yours, Worzel.'

The scarecrow made up his mind in a flash. 'No thank 'ee very much ... I don't think so ... I mean I knows your 'oliness gives ol' Worzel a bit o' stick now an' again, but arter all, what else is a Crowman for? No, I's ready, Mister Crowman ... I's ready ... for whatever you got in store for me.'

The Crowman moved forward into the firelight. 'Are you sure, Worzel?'

'Yes ...' He paused, then frowned. 'I think I'm sure.'

The Crowman breathed a long sigh of relief. 'You've made a wise choice, Worzel. A wise choice and a noble choice.'

'A fool's choice!' hissed the defeated traveller.

'Better a fool than a scoundrel,' replied the Crowman evenly. His voice took on a note of menace again as he gestured towards the courtyard gate. 'Time you left! The gate's behind you.'

The travelling scarecrow-maker backed away cringing, his voice still as grovelling as ever. 'We shall meet again, Master. I thank your Honour for his hospitality. Goodnight, Master Crowman, and goodbye, Master Gummidge.' With his scarecrow slaves at his heels, he slithered away across the courtyard and out into the lane, where the night swallowed him up. The Crowman watched them go, locked the gate, and waved a scrawny hand at the bonfire to extinguish the flames.

'There! That's a bad business well settled. Now, Worzel, you can finish that cake while I remove the bonfire.'

The scarecrow was still confused. 'Remove the bon... the bon... the bon...' he babbled. 'But ain't you a'goin' to chuck me on it?'

'No, Worzel, I am not,' beamed his Master. 'Tonight you were given the choice of good and evil. You chose the good and rejected the evil, even though it would have saved your straw. Good *people* sometimes end up on bonfires – good *scarecrows* never. Now eat up your cake and off to bed with you.'

Worzel Gummidge was not the brightest scarecrow in the world, but he was bright enough not to need telling twice. 'Well I'll be bumswizzled!' he muttered as he galloped indoors.

Half an hour later, when he had finished clearing away the remains of the bonfire, the Crowman made his weary way upstairs, pushed open his bedroom door and groaned with exasperation. For Worzel Gummidge was sitting up in bed, wearing the Crowman's nightcap and nightgown, munching happily on chocolate cake and filling the Crowman's bed with crumbs.

'Worzel Gummidge, what are you doing?'

'You said to go to bed, Mister Crowman, sir,' spluttered the scarecrow indistinctly through a mouthful of cake.

The Crowman roared. 'Not in my bed! And in my night cap! Get up at once! Clear out!'

CHAPTER 3

Ten Heads are Better than One

It was autumn in England. It was raining. A huge flock of screaming herring gulls wheeled and swooped over a vast rubbish tip. Below them, among the bedsteads and old televisions, the bags of mouldering potato peelings and sleeveless cardigans, two cheerful scarecrows scavenged happily. After a few hours burrowing and sniffing and turning-over and digging-out, one of them unearthed a tatty old tin trunk with a shout of triumph. 'T-wor-h-wor-i-wor-s-wor-dip-d-wor-o-wor-dip-zel!' he croaked.

His colleague waved a frayed and knotted length of rope in the air. 'A-wor-n-wor-d-wor-dip-t-wor-h-wor-i-wor-s-wor-dip-zel!'

'T-wor-h-wor-a-wor-t-wor-s-wor-dip-g-wor-o-wor-o-wor-d-wor-dip-zel!'

'Oh arr!' agreed the other, and they stumped off through the slime, dragging their finds after them.

A few weeks later, the tatty old tin trunk was on the other side of the world, in New Zealand, in Pauahatanui, and it was the subject of a great debate. It had survived the sea crossing; it had survived the train journey; it had survived the uncertain suspension of Rooney the Carter's pony and trap. What it had not survived – or rather, what its address label had not survived – was the appetite of Mrs Muldoon's greedy goat.

Outside the Post Office Mrs Patomi the Postmistress stood with her hands on her hips and looked severely at the Carter. 'I blame you, Rooney, for allowing Mrs Muldoon's new billy-goat to scoff the label. Haven't you *any* idea who it was intended for?'

Rooney was a vast, red-faced, stubble-chinned, overgrown goblin of a man with a relaxed approach to life. 'I have not. It was a funny sort of name ... Woozle ... Warzle ... Wizzle ... Something or other. I'm sure I've never come across it anywhere before.'

The postmistress sniffed. 'I believe you there all right. I can't imagine anybody in Pauahatanui laying claim to that battered old thing!'

'Why don't you open it up, Missis, and have a look at what's inside?' suggested Rooney the Carter.

Mrs Patomi shook her head. 'Not until every avenue of identification has been explored, Rooney – Them's official post office rules and regs.'

'I'll tell you what I'll do, Missis,' offered Rooney. 'I'll run next door and fetch Mrs Moon – there's nothing comes or goes round these parts that woman doesn't know about,' and he waddled out of the Post Office without another word.

In the disused stable where he had set up home Worzel Gummidge was experimenting. A pair of old packing cases had been set a few feet apart along one wall, and a builder's plank wobbled between them. On top of the plank wobbled Worzel Gummidge, and on top of Worzel Gummidge, in place of his normal head, was a cabbage.

Mary and Mickey, the two children who had befriended him soon after his arrival in Pauahatanui, sat watching with an air of resignation as the scarecrow set off to walk the plank. The experiment didn't last long: without his head Worzel couldn't see, and after just two paces he tumbled to the dusty ground in a tangle of twiggy arms and legs.

'I told you he was going to fall,' said Mary calmly, cradling the scarecrow's ordinary head in her lap.

'I knew he would before he started,' replied Mickey, not to be outdone.

The headless scarecrow sat up and groped blindly around him. The children crossed the stable to hand him his head. He screwed it back on to his shoulders. 'There we is!' he announced. 'No 'arm done. Tha's proved one thing any road – a cabbage ain't no use fer a balancin' 'ead.'

'Surprise, surprise!' they sang.

Worzel ignored the sarcasm. 'Tha's on account of it ain't got no eyes, see,' he explained. He looked thoughtful. 'A pertater might do orlright – tha's if I c'd find a pertater big enough, o' course. What I really wants is me balancin' 'ead.'

The children looked doubtful. 'I don't believe you've got a balancin' 'ead,' said Mickey.

'Me neither.' Mary agreed.

The scarecrow was indignant. 'Yes I 'as then,' he said huffily. 'I's got a 'ole 'eap o' 'eads – an' I'm goin' to prove it to yer, too – 'cos I's 'avin' my things sent on, ain't I?'

'How can a scarecrow get his things sent on?' asked Mickey.

'You can't write,' pointed out Mary.

'You don't know how to use the phone.'

Worzel Gummidge's head stopped swivelling back and forth between them and he thrust a beaky nose at Mary. ''Oo says I don't? That jus' shows you don't know nuthin'! An' I *can* write, too! I's got a writin' 'ead, so I 'as.' He prodded the boy with a twiggy forefinger to make his point. 'An' a tephylonin' 'ead an' all. I could o' used them, couldn't I, to get a message back to where I comes from to get my things sent on?'

'And did you?' Mary asked.

'No – as a matter o' fack I didn't, 'cos I couldn't, could I? 'Cos I ain't got my 'eads with me – 'cos my 'eads *is* my things,' Worzel finished logically.

'Huh!' said Mickey, unimpressed.

'Don't you huh me, little mister. We 'as all sorts o' ways o' doin' things, us scarecrows 'as. Us c'n talk to birds an' all manner o' creatures. An' tha's what ol' Worzel done, see? 'E tol' a friendly Buller's Mollymawk to pass a message on to a swaller what 'e knows what's 'avin' 'er winter 'olidays in Africky. An' I asked that Buller's Mollymawk to tell that swaller to tell me scarecrow friends back at Scatterbrook as 'ow I was wantin' me things sent on. An' I reckons they must 'ave sent 'em on by now.' Mary and Mickey exchanged a disbelieving glance, but the scarecrow rattled on. 'On'y trouble is, I 'opes as 'ow no daft yewmans don't go pokin' their long noses in where they don't belong. 'Cos if they does they'll get a shock, I reckons. Oh arr – a shock an' a 'alf alright.'

As Worzel Gummidge uttered the words, they came true in the little Post Office on the main street of Pauahatanui. Rooney the Carter knocked the padlock off the trunk, opened the lid, and hauled out one of Worzel's heads.

'Mercy on us!' cried Mrs Patomi, recoiling in horror.

Mrs Moon from next door clutched fearfully at the Postmistress's arm. 'Is the rest of the poor feller in there?' she whispered. 'Or is that all that's left of him?'

'It's not an actual real feller, Mrs Moon,' Rooney explained reassuringly. He scratched his stubbly beard with a noise like mice eating cornflakes. 'If you want my opinion, somebody's carved it out of something.'

Mrs Moon from next door shook her head. 'What sort of a mind would you need to have to fashion a thing like that?' she wondered aloud.

Rooney the Carter grinned hugely and delved into the trunk. 'Whatever sort of mind it was, Missis, it didn't see fit to stop at the one ...' and he hauled out a second head. Mrs Patomi let out another shriek and the two women propped one another up.

'Glory be,' said Mrs Moon, 'That's uglier than the first!'

Rooney nodded, and delved deep into the trunk. 'And there must be a dozen more, at least,' he mused, pulling out another head and comparing it with the others. 'And ... somehow ...' he went on thoughtfully, 'They're all the same to look at ... And yet they're each of them different. Do you take my meaning, Mrs Patomi?'

The Postmistress shook her head. 'I can't even bring myself to look at them!'

Mrs Moon was made of sterner stuff, and stood beside the Carter as he examined the heads. 'I know just what you're getting at, Rooney. They remind me of somebody, but I can't quite put a face to him. Do they ring any bells with you at all?'

'They do, they do...' Rooney nodded, 'But I'm blessed if I can bring him to mind, either.'

Mrs Patomi the Postmistress peeped through her fingers and didn't like what she saw. 'Will you stop it both of you! I just wish to get the abominations off my hands. I'd give a week's wages to know the name of the place they're intended for...'

'The Museum of Folk History, Ma'am, at Waiakikamokau,' said a cultured voice. The three turned with a start to see a dapper little figure standing in the doorway of the Post Office, with a pince-nez dangling across his silk waistcoat and a neat goatee beard sprouting from the point of his chin. He crossed the room, perched his pince-nez on his nose, and took one of the heads from the amused Carter's hands. 'Remarkable ... remarkable ...' He peered deeply into the trunk. 'These are some of the finest examples of primitive folk-culture it's been my pleasure to come across!' He advanced on the Postmistress with a broad smile and an extended hand. 'Allow me to introduce myself – Professor Hagerty, curator of the self-same Folk Museum.' He produced an unstamped letter from an inside pocket. 'And how fortuitous that I should chance to call in here for a postage stamp today of all days.'

'Why is that, Professor?' asked the puzzled Postmistress.

'Because, Ma'am,' said the Professor firmly, 'while I have not the slightest idea where these amazing pieces came from, there can be no doubt that their intended destination was my museum.'

Mrs Moon was impressed. 'Museum pieces, you say?'

'Are they valuable, then?' asked Rooney thoughtfully. His eyes narrowed at the prospect of a reward.

Mrs Patomi the Postmistress shook her head. 'There's no difference if they're worth a fortune or a farthing, Rooney, I'm only glad to see the back of the monstrosities – get them on that trap and off to Waiakikamokau!' She slammed shut the lid of the trunk, and with much 'to-you'ing and 'from-me'ing, Rooney the Carter and dapper little Professor Hagerty managed to manhandle it out of the Post Office and on to the trap.

In the village street the two children, on their way home from Worzel's stable for their lunch, watched curiously. 'What do you think that kerfuffle's all about?' wondered Mary out loud.

'No idea,' shrugged Mickey. 'I'll go and find out,' and he set off towards his mother, Mrs Moon.

'Worzel? Worzel?' A few minutes later, lunch forgotten, the children were back in the stable, jumping with excitement and looking for the scarecrow. He was trying his balancing act again, this time with a large cauliflower where his head used to be. 'Worzel! Come down here! We've found your heads!' cried Mary.

'He can't hear you, Mary,' pointed out the boy. 'Not with a dirty great caulie on his bonce.'

The girl sighed. 'I suppose we'll have to wait until he falls off again.'

'We'll do no such thing!' grinned Mickey, picking up a huge pitchfork twice his own size and advancing on Worzel Gummidge.

The girl looked aghast. 'Michael Moon!'

'It's for his own good,' said Mickey, jabbing the scarecrow

firmly in the midriff with the pitchfork. Scrawny arms and legs flailed in the air as Worzel lost his balance and toppled once more to the dusty floor. The cauliflower tumbled off and rolled across the stable, leaving the headless scarecrow on his knees, scrabbling and groping frantically for his proper head. Mary found it and placed it in his twiggy fingers. He screwed it on and stared around him.

'Oh, 'tis you three, is it?' he said sourly, catching sight of the children. 'I's might ha' guessed. I suppose it were you as gi' me that push were it?'

'Only to break your concentration, Worzel,' Mickey explained.

Worzel Gummidge sniffed. 'Dunno 'bout that – you dang near broke my twigs, so you did – an' you's bin an' bruised my straw! 'Tworn't easy in the fust place – usin' a caulie fer a balancin' 'ead – without you dang titchy yewmans pokin' an' proddin' an' makin' ol' Worzel fall again!'

'That's what we're trying to tell you,' said Mary. 'There's no need to use a cauliflower for a head.'

'You don't know where I c'n lay my 'ands on a big broccoli, does you?' speculated the scarecrow.

'You don't need *any* kind of vegetable. Your other heads have arrived!' she announced.

Mickey nodded confirmation. 'We've seen them. We know where they are!'

Worzel Gummidge scrambled eagerly to his feet. 'Well why the hangment couldn't you 'ave said so in the fust place? Dang aggravatin' titchy yewmans! Come on, then, what we 'angin' about 'ere fer?' and he stomped towards the door, the long-suffering children at his heels.

At a crossroads a few hundred yards out of Pauahatanui the children thumbed an approaching lorry. 'Can you take us to Waiakikamokau?' cried Mary as it pulled up throbbing beside them.

'No problem, kids,' replied the driver cheerfully. 'Hop in.' As the children clambered up the high step into the cab Worzel Gummidge crept out from his hiding place in the hedgerow and hauled himself over the tailboard, arms and legs all over the place. The lorry jerked into gear and rolled forward, and the scarecrow tumbled headlong into a big zinc bath full of disgusting-smelling, sticky, gooey liquid. He stuck a finger in and licked it experimentally. 'Dang me, pigswill!' he announced to no one in particular. ''Tain't bad pigswill, though, as pigswill goes.'

CHAPTER 4

The Little Museum

The commissionaire at the Folk Museum in Waiakikamokau enjoyed his work. By nature he was a thoroughly awkward, pompous, obstructive little man, and to be paid for being awkward, pompous and obstructive made it twice as pleasant. From the window of his poky office he spied the trio coming up the drive, and licked his lips in happy anticipation as he carefully folded his newspaper and stepped out to stop them coming in. 'You can't come in,' he announced with relish as they mounted the steps.

Mickey looked puzzled. 'Why not?' he asked.

'Yer can't come in because I sez yer can't come in – an' I sez so because I've had trouble with your sort before – and apart from that, we're closed!' The commissionaire delivered his well-rehearsed little speech and swayed back on his heels as Mickey looked at his watch. 'Or we will be in a couple of minutes,' the commissionaire added, pointing at a 'Half-Day Closing' sign on the wall.

The scarecrow frowned. 'Suit yersel', yer frosty ol' face-ache,' he replied. 'Anyways, we don't want to come inter yer mouldy ol' museum, does we, titchies?' The children shook their heads firmly.

The commissionaire sniffed. 'Skidaddle, then! We don't want no vagrants hanging around here.'

'We will, Mister – As soon as the other one of us comes out,' finished Worzel craftily.

The commissionaire grinned a sickly grin. 'Oh no – oh no – you don't catch me with that old trick! You're going to tell me

45

that there's four of you, aren't you?' The trio nodded. 'And that the other one's inside there, right?'

'Tha's right,' agreed Worzel cordially.

'And then I tells you to nip inside and fetch him out – and in you goes – and I don't set eyes on you again. Oh no, oh no. I'm not as green as I'm cabbage looking. *You* stop here. *I'll* go in and look for him!' And with that the commissionaire strode off into the quiet little museum.

They waited for a moment on the steps to give him time to get clear. 'Come on, titchies,' the scarecrow ordered, and in they went, avoiding the corridor the commissionaire had taken.

Following a succession of signs and notices they soon found themselves in a large room containing an exhibition of fairground memorabilia. Worzel marched proudly up to a tall glass case where the lifeless Aunt Sally was displayed. 'Tha's my intended in 'er look-through box, that is. My Aunt Sally! I 'spec' she's 'avin' a sulk, I shouldn't wonder ...' He hammered on the glass, to no effect. 'Wake up, Aunt Sally, afore I comes in there an' boxes both yer pretty little ears fer yer! 'Er's my intended, an' I'm 'er intended too. We's both intended to each other, me an' 'er – an' one o' these fine floppoluted days, the Crowman's goin' to officiolate at a ceremony atwixt 'er an' me – 'e's goin' to marry us, me an' Aunt Sally – both of us – together – so's we'll be a proper pair for ever! There now – what've you young titchies got to say to that?' He looked around, beaming proudly, but the children had long since lost interest and had crossed the room to gaze in wonder at a huge calliope, a great fairground steam-organ.

Mickey was awe-struck. 'Hey, Worzel, come and look at this!'

Worzel Gummidge looked across at the children, then back at the lifeless Aunt Sally. 'Sulk on, then! See if I cares, dang ye! 'Appen I'll fine me someone's else – you ain't the on'y turnip in the vegetable patch – not by a long stretch o' garden twine!' he told her grumpily, and marched away to join the children.

'Isn't it great!' breathed the wide-eyed Mary.

Worzel looked, and even he had to agree that it was a wonderful sight. It was a massive calliope, ornately carved and lavishly gilded, with little automata all over the front that played drums and triangles, tambourines and xylophones, accordians and flutes in time with the music. In the very centre there was a life-size figure of a buxom blonde in knee-length velvet green pantaloons, a velvet jacket with a pretty lace collar and black patent-leather shoes with silver buckles, who held a little wooden baton in her lifeless right hand. 'Oh arr!' said Worzel happily, for he loved fairs. 'Tha's one o' they steamy-organs, tha's what that is – they plays music, they does, at fairs an' fêtes an' suchlike. An' the swings swings up an' down; an' the roundybouts goes round an' round; an' my Aunt Sally gets wooden balls chucked at 'er 'ead an' everybody 'as a rare ol' time of it!'

'How do you work it?' asked Mickey.

'*You* doesn't –' said Worzel knowledgeably, pointing to the automata. '*They* works it – an' that there golden-hairdy missis-woman wi' the stick in 'er 'and is the boss o' all o' 'em.' He gazed at her thoughtfully. 'My, my, my, but she's a fair fine figure of a missis-woman an' no mistake– I reckons she'd make somebody a rare ol' wife she would, if they could ever get 'er down off of that there steamy-organ. I wouldn't arf mind a-bein' married to 'er myself.'

Inside her glass case, Aunt Sally heard his distant unfaithfulness, and scowled...

Mickey gazed round the room, spotted the tatty tin trunk and tugged at the scarecrow's jacket. 'Look, Worzel, over there!'

'That's it, Worzel!' echoed Mary, running to open it.

The scarecrow joined them, falling clumsily to his knees, and peered happily into the trunk. 'My oh my – my 'eads' he chortled. ''Ere! 'An jus' look 'ere! 'An' look at this! This one's my 'ead-an'-an-'arf is this 'ead!' He held one up for their inspection.

Mary looked doubtful – it looked very much like his ordinary head. 'What does it do?'

'Why, it's my thinkin' 'ead o' course – what does it look like?'

'But what does it *do*?' pressed Mickey.

'What don't it do! Why, this 'ere 'ead knows everything there is to know – everything what's under the sun, I shouldn't wonder.'

Mickey was as sceptical as Mary. 'It doesn't look to me as if it knows much.'

'Tha's 'cos I ain't got it on, young shaver. Soon as I puts it on, tha's when it starts to think – all sorts of wonderful things it thinks, an' there ain't no stoppin' it once it starts.' He screwed off his ordinary head.

'Bet you it doesn't work,' said Mickey, while Worzel couldn't hear.

'You're probably right,' agreed Mary as the scarecrow screwed his thinking head into place. 'What are you thinking, Worzel?'

The scarecrow blinked.

He thought.

'I think I'll try on some o' these 'ere 'eads,' he declared finally, whipping it off again and putting back his ordinary head.

The children looked at one another with resignation. 'I told you so,' whispered Mickey as Worzel Gummidge rummaged.

'An' look 'ere – this 'ere's my Swedish Circus 'ead – it's called a Swedish Circus 'ead 'cos it's made out o' a swede an' not a mangle-wurzel. An' 'ere's me riddle-me-ree 'ead.'

'What does that one do?' asked Mary, rapidly losing interest.

'Answers riddles o' course.' He held his riddle-mee-ree head nose-to-nose with his ordinary head. 'Why is a scarecrow like a pig-in-a-poke?' he demanded. ''Ow should I know?' he answered himself, tossing it back in the trunk. 'I's got a rememberin' 'ead in 'ere too.'

Mary felt sure she knew what the answer was going to be, but she asked the obvious question just the same. 'Which one's your remembering head?'

Worzel sniggered. 'I don't remember. I knows that this 'un's my magician's 'ead, though ... an' – well I'll be bumswizzled! If it ain't my dancin' 'ead! I's'd forgotten all about this'un.'

'I bet that one doesn't work either,' sneered Mickey.

Mary agreed. 'I don't think any of them work.'

The scarecrow frowned at their lack of faith. 'Oh don't they jus', Missis-Know-It-All! I'll soon show you whether they works or not!' and again he switched heads. As the children watched the scarecrow screwed on his dancing head, clambered to his feet, executed a few clumsy steps, and fell flat on his face.

Mary sighed. 'It's just the same as all the others – none of them does what he says they do!'

Worzel Gummidge nodded. ''Course it don't work! 'Ow's a dancin' 'ead supposed to work – you tell me – when there ain't no music fer it to dance to? You gimme some music, missis, an' I'll show you some dancin', so I will ...' He looked around the room despondently. 'On'y there ain't no music, is there?' As his mournful words fell on the still air there came a strange sighing sound from the steam-organ, as though a distant orchestra was tuning up. The children jumped.

'What was that?' cried Mary.

Mickey frowned and got to his feet. 'It came from over there.'

The scarecrow was delighted. 'It came from out o' the steamy-organ, tha's where it came from.' He scuttled across the room, the children following nervously at his heels, and stood in front of the calliope as it began to wheeze and whirr, faster and faster, until the discordant tuning-up noise became a recognizable fairground tune. Worzel took a few hesitant, tentative steps, then stopped, as the conductress tapped furiously with her baton to bring the music to a shuddering, steaming halt.

'Nein, nein, nein, Vorzel Gummitch!' she announced. 'Vatch der baton alvays und take der time from me!'

Worzel gaped. 'Dang my britches, iffen she ain't been and gone and come to life! 'Oo's you when you're at 'ome, missis?' he demanded. 'An' whyfor don't 'ee talk proper?'

The conductress gave a stiff little bow, her flaxen pigtails quivering stiffly in the air. 'Ven I am at home, Herr Gummitch,' she answered formally. 'I am in der Black Forest, vich is vere I am come from, und I am Trudi von Crotchet – und ven I am not at home, I am here mit der vunderbar steam-orgel und still I am Trudi von Crotchet, der vorld famous celebrated International conductress!' She took a bow to the sound of ghostly applause. It died away on the air and she tapped firmly with her baton to set the cheerful fairground tune playing again. She held out her plump arms to the scarecrow. 'Come, Herr Gummitch, in your arms must you take me und I vill teach you der steps to der tune – ein, swei, drei, veir, so – ein, swei, drei, veir.'

Worzel Gummidge grabbed Trudi von Crotchet clumsily and began to lurch her round the exhibition room, watching his feet and muttering. 'Einy, sweiny, dreiny, veiry ... 'Ow's this, you titchies?' he bawled triumphantly. 'Ol' Worzel ain't 'arf gettin' the 'ang o' things! Einy, sweiny, meeny, miny, mo –'

Aunt Sally threw open the door of her glass case. The crash was clearly audible even over the music, and the children got quickly out of the way as she strode forward. 'H'impertinent 'ussy! I'll teach 'er to twirl around with my h'intended!' She tapped Trudi von Crotchet on the shoulder, but Worzel

Gummidge and Trudi von Crotchet danced on oblivious. 'H'excuse me!' she shouted.

Worzel spotted her. ''Ello, Aunt Sal!' he beamed, delighted. But he did not stop dancing.

Aunt Sally tapped Trudi von Crotchet again, harder this time, and the sound of beechwood knuckles on a boxwood shoulder echoed round the room. 'H'I said h'excuse me,' she repeated loudly. 'Does 'aving painted h'ear-'oles make it 'ard for you to know when someone's talking to you, might I h'ask? *H'excuse me!*'

Worzel Gummidge and Trudi von Crotchet stopped dancing, and the German conductress looked at Aunt Sally with pained surprise. 'Excusen you?' she asked. 'Excuse you for vich? Und vy should I be pleasing to excusen you?'

Aunt Sally stamped a delicate foot. 'Because h'it's a h'excuse-me dance, you h'iggerant h'ill-bred fairground h'ignoramus!'

Trudi von Crotchet was offended, and showed it by clicking her heels and throwing out her chest. 'Und fairground h'ignoramus also to you, ja? Mit knops on!'

'Me? I'm no common fairground appendage, I'll 'ave you know. I was brunged up only at the very best class of fête,' pointed out Aunt Sally with her nose in the air. 'And h'if you don't mind, h'I would like to h'avail myself of the h'opportunity of taking a turn around the dance-floor with my intended.'

Worzel Gummidge was delighted. 'Aunt Sally! You called me your intended! Does that mean that we's a-goin' to get married?' he beamed.

She looked witheringly at him. ''Course it don't – it means I'm considering the possibility.' She looked Trudi von Crotchet squarely in the eye. 'Which means 'ands off as far as you're concerned, you bit of fairground bric-a-brac!'

Trudi von Crotchet stiffened. 'Is this der truth, Herr Gummitch?' she asked. 'Is it engagement to be married you are to this sideshow dumbkopf?'

'I'll dumbkopf you, you steam-organ strumpet!' screeched Aunt Sally. 'I'm genuine memorabilililia, I'll 'ave you know!'

'Oh arr, Trudi – Aunt Sal's my intended right enough – an' I'm 'er intended too – an' right this minute, Aunt Sal,' he went on firmly, ''Ol' Worzel's intending to 'ave a dance with Trudi von Crotchet.'

Aunt Sally was outraged. 'H'intendin' to dance, Worzel? With 'er? You must be off your chump – you ain't seriously h'intendin', I 'ope, to practise the Terps-erpsi-chorean h'art with a woman what's been carved by gypsies and pongs of h'engine-oil and h'axle-grease? Ugh!'

But Worzel was firm. 'I's'll dance with whomsoever I wants to dance with, Aunt Sal, an' neither you nor nobody's a-goin' to stop me!'

There was a mischievous glint in Trudi von Crotchet's eye as she spoke, but neither the scarecrow nor his intended noticed it. She held up a stiff hand. 'Nein, nein, Herr Gummitch,' she declared. 'If to this vormvood-raddled fraulein it is engaged you are, then – jawohl! – it is only right that first dance with her you must. I, Trudi von Crotchet, vill conduct der orchestra.' The children looked at one another suspiciously at this sudden change of heart, but Aunt Sally was delighted.

''Ow h'awfully well-bred of you! Worzel!' she snapped, and the disgruntled scarecrow took her in his arms.

Trudi von Crotchet rapped her baton and the steam-organ struck up the opening chords of a Ländler. 'Ven you are quite ready – Ein, swei, drei, veir –' and the couple began a spirited dance around the exhibition room.

'Do you come 'ere often, Worzel?' asked Aunt Sally formally, making polite conversation as she had been taught.

The scarecrow shrugged. 'As often as I c'n git 'ere, Aunt Sal –' He looked down at his clothes, still damp and reeking from his accidental bath. 'Tha's if I ain't got pigswill down my jacket or cowpats on my boots –' Aunt Sally shuddered, but gripped him tighter as Trudi von Crotchet began to conduct faster and faster, and the music became a gallop. Her eyes widened in alarm as they started to whirl out of control until, with a terrible scream, she flew from the rotating scarecrow's arms and disappeared out of the window.

The music ground to a discordant halt and Worzel tumbled to the floor in a heap of arms and legs. 'Aunt Sally!' he cried in horror.

Trudi von Crotchet was apologetic as she helped the scarecrow to his feet. 'Forgive me, Vorzel – I only vished to make her dizzy – not dispose of her!' They rushed to the window with the children hard on their heels, and peered out. A horrible sight met their eyes, for there, in the road, the travelling scarecrow-maker was loading the stiff form of Aunt Sally on to his cart.

'Oy! Tha's my Aunt Sally, that is!' bellowed the scarecrow. 'You can't do that! You let 'er alone!'

The travelling scarecrow-maker looked across the road at them as he clambered into his cart and took up the reins, his fixed, sinister smile unchanging as ever. 'Oh, but I can, Master Gummidge!' he called. 'And I have!' and he whipped up his bony old nag and clattered away.

'Worzel! Who on earth was *that*?' squeaked Mary.

'Him I do not know, but I sink he is evil, ja?'

Worzel nodded miserably. 'Oh, ja. He's eeliv, right enough. Tha's the Travelling Scarecrow-Maker, tha's 'oo that is.'

'But ... but what does he want with your Aunt Sally, Worzel?' asked Mickey.

A tear trickled down the scarecrow's cheek as he bent to the tatty tin trunk and began to load his heads into a sack. 'I don't rightly know. On'y thing as I does know is, whatever 'e wants 'er for ain't good fer 'er.'

The children glanced at one another in alarm. 'So what are you going to do, Worzel?' Mickey asked.

The scarecrow sniffed, and rubbed a smelly sleeve across his

53

cheek. 'Reckons as 'ow I's'll 'ave to go an' fetch 'er back,' he mumbled.

Trudi von Crotchet clicked her heels and sprang to attention. 'Then I vill accompany you, Herr Gummitch, und be your bodyguard!'

Worzel Gummidge shook his head firmly. 'No, I reckons you's better off where you is. This 'ere's scarecrow business – an' scarecrow business only.'

'Dumbkopf scarecrow! You should haf your head examined. Going alone!'

'I shan't be all alone, exactly.' He patted his sack of heads. 'Not as long as I've got me 'eads to 'elp me.'

Mickey sniffed scornfully, remembering what they'd seen of Worzel's other heads. 'A fat lot of use they'll be.'

''Appen more use than you thinks, young titchy ... It's time I was on my way, I reckons, afore it starts gettin' dark.' Worzel screwed up the top of his sack, tossed it over his shoulder, and headed for the door. Mary glanced inside the tatty tin trunk and called him back.

'You've left one of your heads behind, Worzel.' She held it out to him.

Worzel's face lifted at the sight of the familiar Teutonic-looking head with its monocle, military moustache and spiked helmet. 'Dang me, so I 'as! An' double-dang me iffen it ain't the most important 'ead as I's'll be needin'!'

Trudi von Crotchet licked her cherry-red lips in appreciation. 'Mein Gott und apfelstrudel! Such a fine head did I never see before!'

'Jawohl! This 'ere's my brave 'ead this is. An' that there Travellin' Scarecrow-Maker 'ad best mind 'is magic when I gets it on!' Worzel stuffed it into his sack and strode out into the gathering dusk, his ordinary head held high.

The children looked at one another. 'Come on, Mary. It'll be dark soon. Time we were going, too.'

'Will he be all right, do you think?' wondered Mary nervously.

Mickey shrugged. 'I hope so.'

Alone among the fairground memorabilia, Trudi von Crotchet shook her head slowly. 'Stupid dumbkopf scare-crow! But auf wiedersehn und good luck!'

The little Museum was quiet for a time after the scarecrow and the children had gone. Trudi von Crotchet returned to her proper place on the front of the calliope, and all was normal when the happy little Professor Hagerty entered with the Crowman and scuttled towards the tatty tin trunk. 'You'll be intrigued, I know, Mister Crowman, quite intrigued. They really are the most extraordinary examples of primitive carving I've ever –' He broke off in horror as he flung open the lid and peered in. 'They've gone! They were in here but they've disappeared. But who could have any possible use for them?'

The Crowman smiled a wry smile. 'Worzel Gummidge,' he whispered to himself. 'So you *have* been here.'

The Professor looked up. 'I beg your pardon? Who did you say?'

'I said, I haven't got the faintest idea,' answered the Crowman blandly.

Professor Hagerty wrung his hands apologetically. 'My dear Mister Crowman, I am so sorry to have dragged you all this way for nothing. I'm afraid you've had a wasted journey.' His gaze fell on the steam organ and his face brightened. 'Although – if you're interested in fairground memorabilia – we do have an extremely fine example of a late nineteenth century steam organ ...' He strode towards it, but the Crowman was more interested in the empty case he had just noticed in the far corner, the case which he knew used to contain Aunt Sally. 'Mister Crowman?'

He turned and moved towards the calliope. 'Just coming, Professor, just coming,' he called. 'Worzel, Worzel,' he wondered to himself. 'What torments have you got yourself embroiled in this time?'

Professor Hagerty set the steam-organ going and the two stood for a moment watching the figure of Trudi von Crotchet conducting for all she was worth. Was that a worried frown on her face? the Crowman wondered. Through the open window the music drifted away across the fields, and its faint strains made the miserable Aunt Sally even more miserable as she lay in the travelling scarecrow-maker's filthy hovel amid a tangle of grotesque scarecrow limbs and spare parts...

CHAPTER 5

Worzel Goes to the Fair

For a week Worzel Gummidge tramped the countryside in search of his lost Aunt Sally and the travelling scarecrow-maker. He found nothing. Up hill and down dale he searched, through meadows and woods, along the banks of sweet rivers and in every barn and stable that he passed, but Aunt Sally was nowhere to be found, and he grew daily more depressed.

If Worzel had realized that the travelling scarecrow-maker was growing irritated just as fast as the scarecrow was growing depressed he might not have searched so hard. But he did not know, and every day saw him tramping round and round the farms and fields near Waiakikamokau and Pauahatanui, until one warm morning when he breasted a rise with a stand of tall kauri trees where the raucous rooks nested. He gazed up at them and shook his fist. 'An' caw, caw, caw, again! Pity I ain't got no time now else I'd stop an' give 'ee somethin' to caw about, you pestiferous pesky rooks! But I 'as to go an' rescoo my intended an' give that there Travellin' Scarecrow-Maker what for! An' there ain't nobody nor nuthin' as can stop me from ...'

The scarecrow froze, jaw hanging. He thought he had heard something, some familiar sound ... He waited for a moment, boxed both his ears to make sure they weren't blocked with mud, and waited for another moment, listening intently, but all there was to hear was the soft sighing of the wind and the racket of the rooks. He carried on marching and muttering. 'I sez there ain't nobody nor nuthin' as can keep me from Aunt Sally ...'

He stopped again to listen, and this time his turnip features broke into a great gleeful grin, for on the wind came whispering the faint but unmistakeable sounds of a fairground. 'Nothin' that is exceptin' for a fair! Dang me I knows a fair orl right when I 'ears one – I bet there's upsydownsy swings an' twirly-wirly roundybouts an' such!' and with a lightness in his step he set off in the direction of the music, all thoughts of Aunt Sally and the travelling scarecrow-maker forgotten.

The fairground towards which he was tramping was not yet open. Burly roustabouts stripped to the waist were bolting together dodgem car rinks and huge wheels. Stallholders were busy gluing coconuts into their holders and bending the sights on the rifle range rifles. And in one corner of the fairground a nervous little Professor Hagerty was explaining the workings of the great steam organ – for it was the calliope's unearthly music that the wind had carried to Worzel Gummidge – to a strange-looking character dressed in shabby grey sacking.

'And to turn it off,' said the Professor, 'you just pull this handle here.' He did so, and the music died. 'It's quite simple to operate – on the other hand, the mechanism's very complicated, extremely delicate, and, alas, rather ancient and a trifle worn.' The Professor ran his fingertip over the gilding, and a few flakes of paint detached themselves and drifted lazily down. 'I fear it seems to have developed a tendency, of late, to start playing by itself – we can't locate the fault, unfortunately, try as we may.' He glanced nervously at his silent listener. 'You will treat it with the utmost care?'

The travelling scarecrow-maker's silky voice sent shivers down Professor Hagerty's spine. 'You may rely on me, Professor. I shall handle the machine as carefully as if I had carved every inch of it myself,' he said softly. He moved towards the magnificent calliope and patted Trudi von Crotchet's bottom. 'Beautiful workmanship,' he purred.

Professor Hagerty nodded vigorously. 'Ah! Those Bavarian

craftsmen knew what they were about – it's a very popular exhibit, you know, at all the country fairs and local shows – it's always going on loan.'

'I can well believe it.'

The Professor warmed to one of his favourite topics. 'You see, it not only entertains the visitors who are already here – you can hear a steam-organ across the entire countryside – it draws people to the fair from miles around.'

The travelling scarecrow-maker chuckled, a sinister sound deep in his throat. 'A fact I had already taken into account myself,' he murmured. 'I hired the instrument, Professor, in the belief that it would achieve that very object. And now, Professor, if you will allow me to see you to your car–' and he took Professor Hagerty's arm in one sacking-mittened hand and steered him gently but firmly away from the organ towards the car park.

'But you do promise to take care of it? And you will see that it's delivered safely back to the Folk Museum?' The quavering voice of the Professor continued as they walked. 'And you won't allow anyone not in authority to tamper with it, or chip the paint-work, or meddle with its mechanism–'

As soon as they were out of sight Trudi von Crotchet, furious ever since the travelling scarecrow-maker had patted her bottom, kick-started the calliope into top gear. Music thundered out across the fairground, and the happy scarecrow waddled forwards to drink in the familiar sound. 'My, my, my, – tha's a fine ol' steamy-organ that there is, an' no mistake!' he breathed. He began to conduct. 'I reckon tha's as fine a steamy-organ as that there one they keeps in that grand mooseum what my intended lives in – when she ain't off bein' kidnapped, o' course.' His face froze in horror as he remembered his mission. 'Kidnapped! Dang my best britches! I knowed there was somethin' I was meant to be a-doin' of! Rescooin' Aunt Sally!' He thought of his maker and felt suddenly very nervous. 'An' I's a-goin' to do it too, Your Other-Side-O'-The-World-Ship, juss as soon as I's 'ad a listen to this 'ere steamy-organ!'

From the corner of a nearby caravan the travelling scarecrow-maker watched with evil delight. 'It will draw travellers from miles around indeed,' he hissed, echoing the Professor's words. 'But it seems to have already enticed the one particular customer I had set my sights on capturing!' He picked up a length of heavy chain and began to creep up on the unsuspecting scarecrow.

Worzel Gummidge was carried away by the music, his face one huge smile, his eyes tight shut as the travelling scarecrow-maker swung the chain. There was a dull thud, and a moan, and Worzel opened his eyes in surprise to find Trudi von Crotchet standing beside him, holding a huge German sausage in one hand and slapping it ominously into the palm of the other, a grim expression on her pretty features.

'Well, mulch me up for organic waste in a 'lectric shredder!' he declared happily. 'If it ain't Fräulein Crotchet – an' with a 'andsome bit o' sassidge too! I's partial to a bite o' sassidge, Trudi!' and he leaned forward and bit the end off.

Trudi von Crotchet smiled. 'It is you dat vould der sausage-meat be, Herr Gummitch – had I not struck this dumbkopf mitt der blattwurst!' Worzel Gummidge looked down in surprise to see the travelling scarecrow-maker unconscious at his feet.

'Dang me, it's 'im what's got Aunt Sally an' wants to turn me into one o' they lop-sided scarecrows.' His surprise turned to alarm as the travelling scarecrow-maker began to stir, and with a glance of regret at the remains of the sausage Worzel threw his bag of heads over his shoulder and took to his heels. 'You'll 'ave ter fergive me, Trudi, if I ain't got time to thank 'ee now –'

The travelling scarecrow-maker got to his feet, but he stumbled, and had to be content with calling after the fleeing scarecrow. 'Run, Worzel Gummidge, run! You'll not get far! But first, madam, I'll teach you not to meddle in affairs that don't concern you –' He looked around, bewildered, for Trudi von Crotchet was nowhere to be seen. Nor did he notice that the Steam Organ conductress was using a slightly chewed German sausage as a baton.

As night fell, the scarecrow pulled straw up to ears and settled down for sleep in a draughty barn, counting sheep in his own strange fashion. 'Seven, five, nine, eight, six, an' another one's one, an' another one's eleventeen ... go on, little sheepsies, over you goes, over that hedge ... tha's another one – tha's let me see now? Eleventy twelve that is altogether! Hey, some'ow I think me countin' 'ead ain't workin' proper. Oh well.'

While the scarecrow wrestled with sleep and sheep, the travelling scarecrow-maker paced up and down in his filthy hovel, muttering to himself. In a huge greasy cauldron on a smoky fire a slimy stew simmered with slow, plopping bubbles, like the mud in the hot springs at Rotorua. Aunt Sally lay bound in a corner, more miserable and frightened than she had ever been in her life. 'Curse you, Worzel Gummidge,' hissed the travelling scarecrow-maker. 'But you'll not get off so lightly tomorrow. Come close to here and I'll blind you with magic that the Crowman cannot break – and come close to here you shall.' He looked down at Aunt Sally. 'For I still have just the bait to tempt you –'

He stirred the disgusting–smelling cauldron and spat in it for bad luck. 'Sleep well, Master Gummidge, sweet dreams for tonight, but a cruel world of reality for tomorrow!'

Worzel woke to a beautiful morning. The sun was streaming in through the gaps in the barn wall where planks were missing; flocks of cheeky fantails were singing outside, and cheerful chickens were happily pecking away at the straw of his leg.

'Dang me, 'tis a rare ol' mornin' an' no mistake!' He sat up and stretched. 'An' stop yer strattin' about,' he bawled, batting the squawking chickens off his legs. 'Yes, 'tis a fair ol' mornin' fer doin' somethin' extra special important too, so it is ... if on'y I c'd remember what it was exackly I was agoin' ter do!'

He spotted his bulging sack of heads and dragged it towards him. ''Ello, wha's this ...?' He laid out the heads in a row beside him on the straw. 'Mebbe one o' me other 'eads can tell me what I'm supposed ter do.' He held up his brave head and looked at it with pride. 'Ah, tha'ss my brave 'ead, that is! My, my, my! Come on brave 'ead, tell us. There's somethin' extra important as I 'as ter do.' But his brave head remained silent.

Only a few miles away, the Crowman hunched over his crystal ball and directed all the power of his mind at the scarecrow. '*Aunt Sally*, Worzel! Rescue Aunt Sally!'

Worzel couldn't decide which head to try on, and still had his counting head on when the Crowman's urgent message got through. 'Aunt Sally ... tha's it! Aunt Sally! The Travellin' Scarecrow-Maker's got my Aunt Sally an' I 'as to rescoo 'er. I 'as to rescoo 'er 'ead an' 'er body an' 'er arms an' 'er legs ... 'ow many's that? Tha's an arm an' another arm ... 'ang on, is that one arm too many? I'll start again.'

The Crowman groaned in exasperation at his scarecrow's antics. '*Worzel Gummidge!*' he roared out loud. '*For pity's sake! Take off that ridiculous counting head and get about your business!*'

The message came through so loud and clear this time that the scarecrow thought he was having a brainstorm. He blinked, went cross-eyed, gasped for breath, waggled his fingers in his ears and tried holding his nose. 'Dang me! I 'as to get a move on!' he realized. He looked at the brave head. 'An' I reckons as

I's'll be needin' you afore I's finished, brave 'ead, but not yet awhile – so back in the sack you goes.' He stuffed the brave head in the sack. ''Ere we is – me ornery 'ead.' He took up his ordinary head, placing it carefully on the ground beside him before removing his counting head. ''Ere goes.'

But without a head he couldn't remember where he'd put it and crawled around in the straw on his hands and knees, headless, while his Master sank his head in his hands, hopeless. 'Oh, sometimes I wonder why I bother!' the Crowman moaned.

While Worzel struggled with his heads and his erratic memory, Aunt Sally was stretched out on the splintery work-bench in the travelling scarecrow-maker's filthy hovel. The sacking-clad figure leaned over her, his grin fixed and unwavering. He rapped her forehead cruelly hard with his bony knuckles. 'Solid beechwood – and well seasoned too!' he judged. He ran his long, greasy fingers down Aunt Sally's bare arm. 'And fashioned by a craftsman, I'll be bound. Oh yes, my dear – you'll carve up very nicely – and come in useful as spare parts.'

He locked Aunt Sally's arm in the bench vice and screwed it tight. From a tangled heap of rusy tools he picked up a wicked-looking ripsaw with snaggled teeth, sighted his cold eye along the blade, then paused and put it down again. 'But carving you up, madam, is a treat I must save till later ... First of all I must take care of Scarecrow Gummidge!' He shuffled out, locking the door behind him with a huge rusty key. His horse flinched between the shafts as he clambered up into the cart ...

The Crowman too was setting off at that moment. He squinted up at the sky as if to read the weather, then looked down at a small leather bag with a drawstring neck in the palm of his hand. 'Now then – I hope I haven't forgotten anything,' he muttered, slamming his pick-up door and starting the coughing motor. 'And pray I'm not too late,' he added as he drove off.

Unlike the Crowman and the travelling scarecrow-maker, Worzel Gummidge was lost. He stopped at a crossroads and stared at the sign. As far as he could tell, one arm read '½3 UAKOMAKIKAIAW', while the other seemed to say '½2 IUNATAHAUAP'.

'Wicky-wacky-wocky? Nitty-natty-nutty? What sorta words is they susposed ter be?' he grumbled. 'Don't make sense at all, so they don't ... I reckons I's'd better let my readin' 'ead 'ave a look at them.' He rummaged deep inside his sack, to no avail. 'Dang me! I must 'ave left it in that there barn ... oh well, I'll 'ave to do without it.' He had another go at the signpost. 'Wocky-wacky-wicky,' it said this time, and 'Nutty-natty-nitty.' 'Oh well,' he decided, 'That sounds near enough.' He turned his back on both signs and barged through a thick bank of acacias into a field. 'Let's push on and explore them trees.'

The Crowman's crystal ball had given him a good idea of the direction Worzel Gummidge had taken, and roughly how far away he was, but as he pulled up outside a farmyard he was still rather alarmed to see two small boys throwing stones at one of the scarecrow's heads perched on a wall. 'Just one moment!' he called sternly.

The startled boys turned to face him, feeling guilty and trying hard not to show it. He pointed a long finger at the carved head. 'Might one enquire as to how you came into possession of that ... that article?' he asked politely.

The first boy stiffened up, knowing he had done nothing wrong. 'We found it, Mister.'

'In that barn there, Mister,' his mate added.

The Crowman nodded. His expression softened as he thrust his hand into his trouser pocket and jingled some loose change.

And which would you rather do, I wonder?' he asked with a smile. 'Throw stones or go and buy some sweets?'

The boys exchanged a quick glance and replied in unison. Buy sweets, Mister!'

The Crowman whipped his hand out of his pocket like a conjurer and spun two coins at once high into the air, one to be caught by each delighted boy. 'Then hop it!' he grinned, and they hopped it.

He took down the scarecrow's head and spoke to it through gritted teeth, no grin now on his stern features. 'Worzel Gummidge! Do you imagine I make heads just for you to leave lying around the countryside?' He returned to his pick-up and laid the head carefully on the back seat. 'Still, at least I'm on the right track,' he sighed.

Worzel Gummidge, on the other hand, was not on the right track.

In fact Worzel Gummidge was not on any track at all. At that exact moment the unfortunate scarecrow was deep in the tangled brambles in the heart of the wood, thrashing to and fro for all he was worth. 'Dang pesky branches a-scritchin' an' a-cratchin' at a body!' he bellowed, as they tore away more and more of his precious straw. A rookery rose into flight above his head, wheeling and cawing angrily at his disturbance. 'Caw-aw-caw!' he crowed back. The rooks took no notice, and went on wheeling and cawing. 'An' caw caw caw again!' he repeated. 'Pity I ain't got no time now fer stoppin' an' scarin' you ... you pestiferous pesky rooks! I's got to go an' rescoo my intended an' give that Travellin' Scarecrow-Maker what for! An' there ain't nobody nor nuthin' can stop me from ...'

Once more he froze at a half-heard, half-imagined sound on the wind, this time with his arms and legs outstretched at ridiculous angles on the tangled brambles. The sound died. He decided he must have been mistaken, and pressed on. 'I sez there ain't nobody nor nuthin' can stop me from doin' it ...'

Again he froze, his beady eyes sparkling brightly, for this time there was no mistaking the strains of the calliope. 'Nuthin' that is exceptin' fer a fair! Dang me, them's swings an' roundybouts an' such!' he breathed, imagining the colourful scene. He tore himself furiously free from the brambles and thrashed his way through the undergrowth and out of the wood.

This time the fair was open. All the preparation of the previous day had been completed, and the crowds were beginning to roll up. On the roundabouts adults squealed like children, and the children were as brave as adults as they flew high into the air on the swings. Worzel Gummidge was all eyes; all of him, that is, except for his nose, which was twitching and wrinkling with delight. He followed a familiar old smell to a candy floss stall where he stood with his mouth watering until the proprietor's back was turned. Quick as a flash he plunged a twiggy hand into the swirling bowl and brought it out encased in sugary pink cobwebs, but the proprietor was quicker than he had expected, and gave a mighty, deep-throated bellow. 'Hey! Stop that!' he roared, and once more the scarecrow was on the run. Through swings and merry-go-rounds he dodged, with the angry candy-floss man at his heels, round try-your-strength machines and shooting galleries, until at last he saw some silent dodgem cars under a sign that read 'Out Of Order'. He dived headlong into the nearest car, dragged his scrawny limbs in after him, and grinned with relief as he heard his heavy-footed pursuer go thundering past.

The footsteps faded into the distance, and after a moment's careful waiting Worzel Gummidge risked poking his head up. He looked around nervously and found he was alone in his dodgem car on a deserted and silent rink. He took hold of the steering wheel. 'My, my, my, this is a rum 'un an' no mistake. My own little moty-car.' He cackled with laughter, and then fell silent and frowned with alarm as an unseen hand threw lever and the car began to move. He knew there was something wrong, and it took him almost no time at all to realize what it was. 'Hey,' he squawked, 'Whyfor's it goin' backuds!' The car gathered speed, going round and round in circles, smashing and bashing and crashing into the other cars, until the scarecrow's eyes were crossed and his brain was reeling. 'Oi! Oi! Stop 'em, someone!' he cried in terror. 'This is dizzification! Stop it! 'Elp!'

Round and round went the dodgem car, faster and faster, until the unhappy scarecrow began to turn a delicate shade of green and felt quite sick. Then the hand pulled back the lever again and the car stopped as suddenly as it had started. Worzel Gummidge got out with some difficulty and tried to stagger off the rink, but his turnip head was still spinning, his eyes were rotating in opposite directions with dizziness, and all he managed to do was fall over his own feet. 'Oi'!' he wailed. 'I'm still a-twirlin' an' a-spinnin' ... argh ... like a worsling drervish!' When a kindly stranger came to lend a hand he took it gratefully.

'Oh, my dear sir,' said the stranger, 'You are in a state.' He led the scarecrow to the edge of the rink.

'I yam, I yam!' Worzel Gummidge moaned.

'The machinery must be at fault. Dangerous – must be put right – and so must you sir! To the hospital.'

''Ostipal!' blinked the scarecrow, still quite unable to focus.

The stranger insisted. 'Where we can give you the loving care and attention you need ...' He helped Worzel with his sack of heads. 'Here, I'll take those ... Too heavy for you.'

''Old on!' gurgled the confused scarecrow, just managing to remember what was in the sack. 'Tha's got me brave 'ead in it!'

The stranger laughed. 'Brave head! You don't need no brave 'ead. Splendid fellow like you!' and he bundled the still-twirling, still-cross-eyed Worzel into the back of his cart, took up the reins in a sacking-mittened hand, and cracked the old pony on the flanks.

CHAPTER 6

Worzel to the Rescue

The Crowman was hard on his scarecrow's heels. At the crest of a little hill he stopped and stood up in his old pick-up, his keen eyes and ears straining for a clue. 'Now ...' he mused, 'Which way to go from here?' The faint sounds of the steam organ drifted up to him on the wind and he nodded slowly. 'A fair ... a fair ... I suppose that's as likely a place as any.' He sat down again, hammered the car into gear, and rolled downhill.

For half an hour he wandered sadly round the fairground, unable to find any trace of the scarecrow, past the deserted dodgems and the candy-floss man, past the roundabouts and hoop-la stalls, until he came at last to the coconut shy. 'All the fun of the fair ...' called the brawny stall-holder, 'Three balls a go! Who's next for the shy?'

With a terrible shock the Crowman caught sight of the balls the stall-holder was offering: they were Worzel's heads! 'One down wins you any coconut on the stall,' roared the huge man, the heads like marbles in his vast hands. 'Any more for any more?'

The Crowman rushed up to him. 'Those heads! Those heads!' he cried. 'Tell me, where did they come from? It's important.'

The stall-holder glanced down at him from his superior height. 'None o' your business!' he announced gruffly.

The Crowman was not to be brushed off so easily. 'It certainly is my business! I made those heads – all of them.'

'And a pretty gristly lot they are,' the stall-holder sniffed. He raised his voice and carried on shouting. 'Now roll up! Roll up! One down wins you a coconut!'

The Crowman tugged at his sleeve. 'I must know! Tell me! Where did you get them?'

'Well if you really must know, I bought 'em off the Travelling Scarecrow-Maker, legit, not a half-hour since! Now clear off! You're gettin' to be a nuisance,' he threatened.

'But those heads weren't his to sell!' protested the Crowman. 'They belong to me ... Well, not to me exactly,' he admitted.

The stall-holder was getting annoyed. He shoved his sweaty face up close to the Crowman's. 'Didn't you 'ear? You're gettin' to be a nuisance. Now shove off, buster, afore I shoves you meself!'

'But I –' There was something in the Crowman's voice that showed his genuine concern and softened even the rough stall-holder's heart.

'Now look ... I'm not a mean man ... So take one of these 'orrible 'eads as a souvenir.' He tossed across the brave head. 'Now go on! 'Oppit!' The Crowman saw that there was no more to be done, and sadly moved away, cradling the head, as the stall-holder continued to holler. 'Now roll up, roll up! Knock off an 'orrible 'ead and you wins a coconut! Every one a winner!'

Worzel Gummidge's ordinary head was at that moment an 'orrible 'ead, for the bumping and bouncing of the racing pony and trap had made the whirling and dizziness worse. He peered about him through blurry eyes as they came to a halt. "Ere! What's goin' on? This 'ere don't look like no 'ostipal!'

The travelling scarecrow-maker smiled his sinister smile as he helped the scarecrow down. 'Clinic, sir,' he lied. 'Fashionable clinic, where your every need will be met.'

'An' stop this 'ere twistlin'?'

'Definitely!' said the other as he thrust Worzel through the arched front door.

The scarecrow landed heavily on a bare stone floor, and lay

69

for a moment with his senses reeling as a key grated in the lock behind him. 'Worzel!' cried a familiar voice, and he pulled himself to his feet to find the pitiful figure of Aunt Sally crouched sobbing in a corner, with one of the travelling scarecrow-maker's hideous creations standing immobile, guarding her.

'Dang me, Aunt Sal – I knowed all along I's'd find 'ee afore I'd done!'

Worzel's intended was so miserable that she didn't even have the strength to complain about how long it had taken him to find her. 'What's happening, Worzel? What's to become of me?' she whimpered.

Worzel put his beady eye to the keyhole, ignoring the immobile monster on guard, and peered out into the yard, where the travelling scarecrow-maker was hunched over a pedal-driven grindstone, sharpening an ugly-looking carving knife and chuckling evilly to himself. Worzel turned to Aunt Sally and shrugged. 'I reckon what's to become o' you, Aunt Sally, is the same as what's ter become o' me. An' that's 'im out there a-sharpenin' o' 'is knives ter do it to us.'

'Do what?'

'Chop us up, o' course. An' use our arms an' legs an' that ter make more on 'is lop-sided scarecrows.' He pointed at their guardian. 'Like 'im there.'

Aunt Sally was appalled. 'Not me, Worzel? Surely 'e wouldn't chop me up, would 'e? I mean, 'e could chop *you* up seein' as 'ow you're just a common scarecrow. But not *me*, Worzel – a priceless antikew – 'e wouldn't dare!' Doubt crept into her mind and she crept closer to Worzel. 'Would 'e?'

'I reckons as 'ow 'e will, Aunt Sal. Both on us. But we ain't beat yet – we'll do what I allus does when I ain't got me brave 'ead on!' he announced boldly.

'What's that?'

'Run away – I reckons I's the bestest runner-awayer there is,' he boasted.

Aunt Sally snorted. 'Don't talk ridicerlessless! The door's locked tight and the window's barred and ...' she pointed at their hideous guard. 'And even if they weren't – What about him?'

The scarecrow marched across the room. 'I ain't a-frighted o' 'im. Even without my brave 'ead. Watch this!' and he stuck out his tongue. The ugly great scarecrow's eyes flashed with anger, but he couldn't move, and Worzel stuck his thumb to his nose and waggled his fingers in his face. 'Nyaah ... nyaah ... nyaah ... Can't touch me, silly ol' sassidge!'

'Oh, Worzel!' gasped Aunt Sally, genuinely impressed for once.

Worzel Gummidge explained. 'See, Aunt Sally? 'E can't do nothin'. None of 'em can – not when it's light. They can on'y move about when it's dark. The Crowman tol' me. Come on.'

'Come on where to? We're still locked in,' she pointed out unhappily.

'Come on up the chimbley.'

Aunt Sally was quite horrified. She had never come on up a chimney in her life. 'Up the chimbley?' she gasped, but the determined scarecrow shoved her firmly up through a great downpour of soot.

They crawled on to the roof as black as crows, and paused for a moment to scrub their eyes so that they could spy out their next move. Luckily their captor's filthy, ramshackle little hovel was only a single-storey building, and they weren't far from the ground. They peered over the edge, spotted the travelling scarecrow-maker in the yard below, still sharpening his evil-looking knife on the grindstone, and ducked back out of sight again. Worzel Gummidge dragged Aunt Sally across the roof to the opposite side and glanced over. ''Tain't far ter drop, Aunt Sally. An' there's plenty o' nice soft mud ter land in,' he promised her. She opened her rosebud mouth to protest, but too late – the scarecrow's sturdy boot caught her square in the backside and she flew through the air to land with a splat in a pool of thick mud. A second later, the scarecrow landed beside her, and scrambled unsteadily to his feet. 'So far so good. Come on, we ain't out o' the mud yet!' he pointed out.

Dragging the filthy figure of Aunt Sally behind him, Worzel set off through the mud, only to freeze in horror as the travelling scarecrow-maker suddenly appeared round the side of his hovel with two of his monstrous creations. 'Not so fast Master Gummidge ... Nor your wooden lady-friend!'

The scarecrow gibbered with fright. 'I ... er ... I was ... going to ...'

The travelling scarecrow-maker sneered. 'You are going nowhere! Neither of you.' He turned to his terrible companions. 'Take 'em back!'

'They can't take us back,' said Worzel Gummidge defiantly. 'They can't do anything 'cos they can't move ... They ...' His voice tailed off as the two huge scarecrows began to lumber forward.

'Can't they?' The travelling scarecrow-maker smiled evilly. 'They will go wherever I tell them ... Night *or* day!' And he sent them forward with a wave of his sacking-mittened hand.

'*Stop*!' The Crowman's voice cut like a whip through the dank air. He stood, tall and powerful, at the edge of the trees, a piece of gnarled and twisted old oak twig in his outstretched hand.

The travelling scarecrow-maker turned his sinister smile on the new arrival and nodded slowly. 'Ah,' he breathed, 'I wondered when your Highness would appear. But I don't know what for. There's little you can do now.'

'*I can do enough*,' replied the Crowman grimly. He pointed his outstretched twig at the two monsters, and in a strong, clear voice began to chant;

Plague, pestilence, misery,
Flood, flame and foul weather ...
By all that is good within me ...
I bid thee hold no more together!

A distant rumbling built up behind his words to climax in a huge clap of thunder as he snapped the twig. The two monster scarecrows slowly began to disintegrate, layers of sacking peeling off and falling in tatters to the muddy ground, the straw of their bodies blowing away on the soft wind, until there was no more left of them but two pathetic piles of dust.

The scarecrow cackled with delight. 'My, my, Your Majesty! You's disigrinated them!' he chortled.

'I have indeed,' nodded the Crowman grimly. He held out a head to Worzel Gummidge. 'And now you must play your part.'

Worzel Gummidge's eyes sparkled as he caught sight of the familiar monocle, the spiked helmet and military moustache. 'Oh my, oh my! It's me brave 'ead!' He grabbed it eagerly. 'Jus' you wait a minnit an' I'll show you wha's what!'

The travelling scarecrow-maker sneered. 'You? Don't be ridiculous!'

'Ridicilous, am I? Jus' you watch!'. The scarecrow swiftly unscrewed his everyday head and put on the brave head. It would have been more impressive if he had put it on properly.

As it was, Aunt Sally raised her eyes to the skies and squawked at him. 'Idiot! You've got it the wrong way round!'

'Oh ... sorry ... sorry, Aunt Sal.' He quickly swivelled it to the front and turned a cold eye on the travelling scarecrow-maker. 'Ja! Gut! Now, mein untermensche! ... You will get out ... Raus! Raus!'

'Fool! You can do nothing! Nothing!' laughed his opponent, but his laughter stopped suddenly as the newly-brave scarecrow grabbed a wicked-looking pitchfork and advanced.

'Mit my brave 'ead you will retreat, you dumbkopf! Go for ever ... dupple dumbkopf! Tot! Or I will chop you to little pieces ... into kleine bits of liver ...' As he advanced, Aunt Sally gazed at her scarecrow transformed into a hero, and clasped her hands to her bosom. 'You are a cowardy custard!' Worzel went on, 'Eine figling! Leave this place for ever!'

The travelling scarecrow-maker started to shimmer and sparkle like one of his own dolls, and a swirl of blue smoke enveloped his body. There was a sudden flash like bright white lightning, and he was gone.

'Oh, Worzel, Worzel!' cried Aunt Sally ecstatically.

The Crowman breathed a sigh of relief. 'Well done, Worzel Gummidge, well done. And now, if you please, I think you had better let me have your brave head for safe keeping ...'

The scarecrow drooped. 'But Mister Crowman, sir ... I might need it for an emergency ... 'e might be back,' he argued.

'He probably will, Worzel,' agreed the Crowman calmly. 'But I think I know how to deal with him ... Now, the head, please.' He held out his hand.

Worzel Gummidge tried wheedling. 'But your 'oliness, jus' fer today ... So's I can protect me Aunt Sally.'

The Crowman softened, and laughed. 'Very well, Worzel, just this once. But wear it well and bring it back safely to me.'

'Oh, I will, your generosity, I will!' he promised.

Worzel Gummidge and Aunt Sally followed the Crowman round the corner of the deserted hovel and across the yard to the grassy track where he had parked his old pick-up. 'And now,' he announced, 'I must see if I can retrieve the rest of your heads from the fair. My heads, targets in a coconut shy ... Oh dear, oh dear.' Worzel watched the Crowman drive off, waving wildly till he was out of sight, but Aunt Sally only had eyes for her brave new scarecrow hero.

He turned to her and clicked his heels impressively. 'Und now, mein Aunt Sally, it is time for me to go,' he declared. To her surprise and delight he lifted her hand to his lips and kissed it.

'Go, Worzel?' she gasped. 'Go where?'

He snapped to attention and saluted. 'To the war, kleine puppe ... Vere ich mussen fight.'

Aunt Sally was bewildered. 'Fight? Fight who?'

'Ze enemy ... zere is always ze enemy ... Zey must be

vankvished just as I vankvished der Travelling Scarecrow-Maker ... Tot! So au-widersin mein scoene liebe!' He saluted again, did a parade-ground turn, tripped up slightly and marched away.

Aunt Sally's little legs went like piston-rods as she tried to keep up. 'Worzel!' she squeaked. He kept on marching, across the yard and out into the lane. 'Worzel! Worzel Gummidge!'

He halted, stamping his boots into the soft grass, turned again, clicked his heels and looked at her in surprise. 'Ja?'

'You're not leaving me, are you? Leaving me *here*?

'Ja ...'

'But not ...' She gestured at the travelling scarecrow-maker's hovel. 'Not in this awful place.'

The brave scarecrow shrugged. 'Ja ... Why not? Warum?'

'Because you can't ... It isn't ... gentlemanly,' she explained, trying to think of excuses for him to take her with him. ' 'Specially as you're an Hofficer,' she tried. She saw that it was having no effect, and played her trump card. 'An' anyway, I'm your intended.'

It was the most difficult thing in the world for her to say, but it had its effect on the scarecrow. He froze with pleasure, then screwed the monocle more tightly into his eye and beamed down at her. 'Mein intended? Did you say mein intended?'

Aunt Sally nodded frantically, her fingers crossed behind her back. 'Yes, yes, I did! But just take me away from here.'

Worzel Gummidge would have liked to get it in writing. 'Mein intended,' he repeated. 'For ever und ever?'

As desparate as she was, even Aunt Sally couldn't go that far. 'Well, for ever and ever's a long time,' she pointed out. 'Let's just say for this afternoon.'

It would have to do. He clicked his heels, gave Aunt Sally a little bow, and offered her his arm. 'Gut enough!' he conceded. 'Kom mit!' She took his arm, and they marched off together down the green lane.

CHAPTER 7

Slave Scarecrow

That night, the tired Crowman strolled for a while around his cobbled courtyard, listening to the hypnotic splashing of the mill-wheel and the distant roar of the ocean. He was a little easier in his mind after having rescued Worzel Gummidge and Aunt Sally, and after having apparently defeated the travelling scarecrow-maker, but there was still something about the evil little figure that he couldn't quite put his finger on. 'Something about his attitude towards me,' he muttered, frowning. 'He seeks to challenge my authority, my power, and yet he is servile, respectful, as though ... As though I really don't know what,' he yawned. The warm night air had made him sleepy. As the first fingers of light from a new moon slithered through the giant ponga trees he heard the distant chimes of the church clock in the village, and hauled out his huge pocket watch on its heavy gold chain. 'Midnight,' he sighed. 'High time I was abed. My mind will be clearer in the morning.'

He pulled on a long white nightshirt and cap, and clambered into his creaky old four-poster. On the bedside table his crystal ball was swirling with milky clouds. He passed his hand over it and the clouds cleared to reveal the familiar beaky nose of the scarecrow poking out from beneath a moth-eaten horse-blanket on the floor of the stable. The Crowman smiled, satisfied that all was well, and settled back in his bed. In only a moment he was deep in a dreamless sleep.

In the stable, just as the Crowman had seen, Worzel Gummidge was asleep, but his was no dreamless sleep. Aunt Sally's new warmth towards him after his duel with the travelling scarecrow-maker had touched his scarecrow heart, and his dreams were rich and lively. 'Aunt Sally ... Aunt Sally ...' he mumbled indistinctly, eyes tight shut. 'You's made me the 'appiest scarecrow in all the wide world, Aunt Sally.'

He gave a contented snort, and a huge smile spread across his turnip face as, in his dream, he walked proudly up the aisle towards the waiting Crowman, Aunt Sally a picture in white lace on his arm. For he was dreaming of what he had always wanted – his marriage to Aunt Sally! 'From this 'ere day forward,' he echoed as the Crowman prompted him, 'For 'avin' cake or not 'avin' cake, in good temper or in bad temper, until being chucked on a b-b-b-bonfire do us part ...'

He thrashed uncomfortably under his blanket for a moment at the thought of the bonfire, then settled again and looked forward to the best part ...

But while scarecrow and Crowman slept, others were awake. There was the faintest of creaks as the courtyard gate swung open, and from the shadows the travelling scarecrow-maker stepped softly forward into the bright moonlight. He had returned, just as the Crowman had suspected he would, and at his heels lumbered two more of his zombie-like scarecrow slaves, the horrible little talismans that gave them temporary life sparkling at their throats. He paused at the edge of the courtyard beside the slowly-turning mill wheel and looked up at the Crowman's bedroom window. His fixed smile was as sinister as ever as he beckoned one of the scarecrow slaves forward and took from the dull creature a wickerwork cat basket within which something shifted nervously.

The travelling scarecrow-maker was a million miles away from Worzel Gummidge's dream. There, the formal part of the ceremony was over, and he and his new bride were sitting down at last to the wedding feast, at a long table laid with every variety of cake and gâteaux and éclair known to the art of cookery. At the head of the table, right in front of the happy couple, was the *pièce de resistance*, the cake to end all cakes, a wonderful white wedding cake, three tiers high and so wide that its base overlapped the table on either side by several inches. The crisp white icing was decorated with little pink bows and hearts, and models of Worzel Gummidge and Aunt Sally made of spun sugar beamed happily from the top of the topmost tier. On a signal from the Crowman that the feasting could begin, Aunt Sally grabbed the top tier in both hands, Worzel did the same with the next – and larger – tier, and they began to cram their mouths so full that they could barely munch.

The Crowman stirred. For a moment he gazed sleepily at the ceiling, then in an instant he snapped wide awake, suddenly aware that he had heard a sound. He lay quite still, hardly breathing, listening to the sounds of the night; 'Was it simply an owl?' he asked himself. He sighed, knowing that it was not, threw aside the bedclothes and padded silently to the window.

There was nothing to be seen in the courtyard; when one of the scarecrow slaves had stumbled, waking the Crowman, the travelling scarecrow-maker had thrust both his ghastly creations angrily into the shadows of the workshop, out of the Crowman's sight. But he had known how clumsy his slaves were, had known that they could not be relied upon for silence, and had come prepared. As the Crowman pushed up a stiff sash window to peer out, the travelling scarecrow-maker took from the wickerwork cat-basket a battle-scarred old tabby and tossed it out into the moonlight, where it yowled once and sped off into the darkness.

The Crowman saw, and heard the caterwauling, and laughed at his fears. 'Just a cat. Nothing more.' He slid shut the window and returned to his bed. In the crystal ball on his bedside table the image of Worzel Gummidge still beamed contentedly from his dream. The Crowman smiled down at him, for he had a very strong suspicion that he knew exactly what the scarecrow was dreaming of. He pulled up the covers again, and was soon deep in his own dreamless sleep.

The travelling scarecrow-maker was patient. Not until the church clock in Pauahatanui struck three, and he was sure that nothing would wake the sleeper, did he creep silently into the Crowman's room. His beady eyes flickered nervously from side to side until he found what he was looking for.

He started forward.

The Crowman stirred in his sleep.

The travelling scarecrow-maker froze.

The Crowman turned over, and was still again. Not daring even to breathe, the grey visitor reached out a sacking-clad mitten and picked up the crystal ball. He stared at the image of the slumbering scarecrow, and crept out into the night again, silent as a grey shadow.

In the courtyard he stood for a moment in the moonlight, clutching his precious trophy, then tossed it gleefully up into the air and caught it again ...

The effect on Worzel was immediate. He tossed and turned, thrashed violently on his straw bed, and called out in alarm. ''Ere, let me down, what you think you're a'doin' of?' He woke with a start and sat up, relieved to find himself back in the familiar surroundings of the stable. 'What a norful nightmare!' he moaned. 'Musta been that there cheese an' sassidges an' them slices o' cake an' a few biscuits an' a happle an' some potatey crisps an' a meat pie an' cups o' tea an' limmonade an' that what I 'ad for me supper ...' Having come to what was, for him, a perfectly reasonable conclusion, he settled back in the straw, looking forward to returning to his dream.

In the courtyard, the travelling scarecrow-maker stared into the crystal ball and hissed with delight. He knew where the scarecrow was! Once more he tossed the shining sphere into the air ...

As the crystal ball spun, so did the scarecrow. He sat up again, bewildered, and rubbed his stomach. 'Ignigestion, that's what it is, Worzel,' he told himself. 'Ignigestion ... through eatin' that happle ...'

Having got what he wanted, the travelling scarecrow-maker left the courtyard. But now he was empty-handed, and gentle circles rippled on the green surface of the millpond ...

'Glug glug glug ...' went the baffled scarecrow. His ears popped as though they were full of water, and he shook his head to clear them. He began to get angry with himself for wasting so much good dreaming time awake. 'What you talkin' about, Worzel Gummidge – glug glug glug? You ain't right in the 'ead, so you ain't. Get yerself back to sleep an' finish that there weddin' cake.'

Armed with the knowledge he had got from the Crowman's crystal ball, the travelling scarecrow-maker soon found the stable. He leaned over the sleeping scarecrow and whispered his name. 'Worzel ...' The scarecrow stirred, and in his half-asleep state thought of his maker. The travelling scarecrow-maker repeated his name, louder now. 'Worzel Gummidge!'

'Was that you, your back-in-Englandness?' murmured Worzel as he slowly drifted up to wakefulness. His opening eyes fell on the familiar photograph pinned roughly to the wall. 'Funny, I didn't see your lips move. I never knewed you were one o' them there ventrilenti ... ventrilinkli ... ventri ...' He turned, and for the first time caught sight of the travelling scarecrow-maker. The two scarecrow slaves loomed over him menacingly, brandishing ugly sickles in their misshapen hands. The travelling scarecrow-maker extended a bony finger towards his victim and beckoned. Worzel Gummidge pulled the horse-blanket up to his chin and began to gibber with fright. 'Wer-wer-wer-wer-what you want?'

'I want you, Worzel Gummidge. Come,' the travelling scarecrow-maker replied.

'Cer-cer-cer-cer-come where?'

'You'll see.'

'Ber-ber-ber-ber-but I ain't finished my sleepin' yet,' the unhappy scarecrow pointed out.

The travelling scarecrow-maker laughed. 'There'll be time enough for sleep. All the sleep a scarecrow could wish for. Come,' he repeated.

'Whaffor? Wot you want of poor ol' Worzel, Mister?'

'Not Mister, Worzel Gummidge,' snapped the other. '*Master*.' He lost patience, and with a violent sweep of his arm waved the scarecrow slaves forward to seize Worzel Gummidge. 'And hurry! There is little time left.'

The time ran out just as the travelling scarecrow-maker, cruelly whipping his poor old pony, turned his clattering cart through the gateway and into the yard outside his filthy hovel. As the scarecrow slaves stood either side the door, a cock crew, and they froze, lifeless again at the approach of the first thin light of dawn.

The travelling scarecrow-maker hissed a sigh of relief. Just in time! He prodded a sack in the back of the cart with a bony forefinger. 'Good morning, Worzel Gummidge,' he murmured softly. There was a muffled, frightened reply from the sack. 'A scarecrow that can walk by day. What I've always dreamed of!'

The Crowman woke at cock-crow, and quickly dressed. From the highest shelf in the cool larder beside his kitchen he took down a weighty cake-tin, prised off the lid, and squinted inside. What was inside was only a poor relation of the wedding cake in Worzel's dream, a cake barely a foot across and four inches deep, clumsily but lovingly iced by the Crowman himself. But this cake was real, and on the top was pink icing that read 'Happy Birthday Worzel's Head' ...

Bearing it proudly before him he set off for the stable in high good humour, humming 'Happy Birthday to you,' but a frown crossed his face as he found the stable doors thrown open wide and a huge pig happily rooting round in the mud. 'Careless

Scarecrow,' he grumbled, shaking his head. 'That pig could have eaten your head and you'd never have known about it.' He prodded the pig with the toe of his boot to move it aside. 'Come on, Master Porker – about your business!'

The pig shambled off and the Crowman strode in. He stopped beside the humped shape under the horse-blanket, cleared his throat, took a deep breath, and in a quavering voice began to sing.

'Happy birthday to you
Happy birthday to you
Happy birthday dear Worzel's head
Happy birthday to you ...!'

There was no response. The Crowman grew rather irritated. After all the trouble he had gone to make the cake ...! 'Come along, Worzel – rise and shine! Your very first birthday in New Zealand and I want you to make the best of it ...' He paused, and set down the cake. 'Very well, then – when it's your legs' birthday or your arms' birthday or your stomach's birthday, no cake for you!'

Thoroughly annoyed by now, he hauled off the horse-blanket. 'Up you get, you idle scarecrow!' A terrible sight met his eyes. 'Bless my soul!' Beneath the horse-blanket lay a sack of potatoes for a body and a crudely-carved pumpkin like a hallowe'en mask for a head. The Crowman's eye fell on the photograph of his Master, the Crowman of all Crowmen, that had hung lopsidedly on the wall. It was now on the floor, and torn into two. He slowly picked up the two pieces and held them together. 'I've let you down,' he whispered sadly. 'You gave Worzel into my custody and I've let you down.'

With leaden feet he turned and made his way home, the cake a dead weight in his arms.

Worzel Gummidge had not forgotten his head's birthday, but he couldn't see much chance of celebrating it. In the travelling scarecrow-maker's filthy hovel he was securely tied to a chair, watching his new master frying breakfast in a huge greasy pan over a smoky brazier.

'Are you partial to bacon and eggs, Worzel Gummidge?' asked the thinly-smiling figure.

He nodded eagerly, his mouth watering. 'I am that. Partial as partial, I am, to bacon and eggs.'

'Fried slice?'

'Ooh, arrr! Nearly as nice as a slice of cake, a fried slice is.'

'Mushrooms? Tomatoes? Fried potatoes? Baked beans?'

Worzel started to dribble. The smell was delicious and his imagination supplied the taste. 'Jus' some o' each ... Coo, my mouth's waterin' so much I c'd drown a rat in it.'

'Sausages?'

'Sassidges? I lives and breathes for sassidges!' He stared greedily as the travelling scarecrow-maker heaped the greasy pile onto a grubby chipped plate. ''Ere – tell you what. As it's my 'ead's birthday today, what about instead o' three sassidges, *two* sassidges!'

'Another sausage? By all means, Worzel Gummidge ... There! A breakfast fit for a King!' He set the tempting plate on a rickety table a few inches below the scarecrow's quivering nose.

''Tis that, an' no mistake. It's a breakfast an' an 'arf, that there is. Only thing is, bein' trussed up like a chicken, I don't rightly know 'ow to eat it.'

The travelling scarecrow-maker raised his eyebrows in mock-surprise. 'Eat it, Worzel Gummidge? *You're* not going to eat it! I'm going to eat it!'

Worzel's face crumpled, and his lower lip began to tremble. 'What an 'orrible, 'eartless thing to do to a pore scarecrow!'

'Ah, but that's because I'm a horrible, heartless, cruel, travelling scarecrow-maker, Worzel Gummidge. But I have a purpose in my poor little joke. I was showing you how I like my breakfast – and tomorrow, and the next day, and for as long as I shall spare you, *you* will cook my breakfast.'

83

Worzel Gummidge looked defiant. 'Ah, well that there I can't, see? Because I promised the Crowman faithful I'd never go near no fer-fer-fer-'

'Near the fire? But you don't obey the Crowman now, Worzel Gummidge – you obey me.'

'Oh no I doesn't, an' I ain't goin' to cook you no breakfuss.'

The travelling scarecrow-maker shrugged. 'Please yourself, Worzel Gummidge. I can always make do with turnip stew.'

'Turnip stew? 'Ere, what you mean, turnip stew?' Worzel struggled in vain with his strappings. 'You let me go – I wants to go 'ome!'

'But you *are* home, Worzel Gummidge. Don't you understand? Like all my scarecrows, you're my scarecrow slave,' said the travelling scarecrow-maker. He pronged a sausage, ran it under Worzel Gummidge's tormented nose, and began to munch it.

The Crowman had forgotten all about breakfast. He scampered to and fro around his house and his workshops, searching frantically for his missing crystal ball. 'Oh dear, oh dear, where is my crystal ball? So absent-minded ... Now did I take it to bed to keep an eye on Worzel, or did I not? And if I did, why *didn't* I keep an eye on Worzel? I shall never forgive myself ...'

Picking things up and putting things down, peering into boxes and baskets, his search took him out into the courtyard where the children were kicking a football around beside the still millpond. 'It can't have vanished into thin air,' he muttered. His eye fell on a tiny shred of grey sackcloth caught on the latch of the gate, and his expression darkened. 'Worse than I thought,' he declared. 'Worse than I thought.'

He peered into the dustbin at the precise moment the football sailed in, and looked up in surprise at Mickey and Mary, as though seeing them for the first time.

'Can we have our ball back, please, Mister Crowman?' asked Mickey politely, as the Crowman picked the ball out.

An idea occurred to him. 'All in good time. I want you to help me find something ...'

'Worz – I mean, your scarecrow?' Mary corrected herself.

The Crowman shook his head. 'No, I think I know where my scarecrow is, more's the pity. I'm looking for a ball.'

'You can't have that one,' said Mickey reasonably. 'It's ours.'

'No – it's very much like this, but it's made of glass.'

'A glass football?' Mary looked disbelieving. 'It'd break.'

'No, it's not a football, it's – well, it's for looking in. You'll know it if you find it, children. Look on the rubbish tip.' They started to set off, but he called them back. 'And in all the dustbins ... And – and in the quarry ... And in the fishpond but don't get your feet wet.' Again they started to leave and again he called them back. 'And children ... You'll need lollipops to sustain you ...' He gave them a coin each. 'Off you go. There'll be a reward, mind!' It was all the encouragement they needed. They scampered out of the courtyard, football forgotten, and into the lane.

As the hungry Worzel watched, the travelling scarecrow-maker mopped the last morsel of eggy grease off his plate with a wodge of bread and butter, and munched it contentedly. 'An excellent breakfast,' he congratulated himself. 'And now to work, Worzel Gummidge.'

'Ent you forgotten somethink, Mister?' asked the scarecrow.

'My toast and marmalade? I've had sufficient, thank you.'

'Ar, but ol' Worzel 'asn't. When does I get my breakfuss?'

The travelling scarecrow-maker started to untie the knots holding Worzel Gummidge prisoner. 'But you're a scarecrow – a thing of twigs and straw. Scarecrows don't need breakfast, Worzel Gummidge.'

'They doesn't *need* it,' he agreed, 'but they *'as* it.'

'*Not in this household.* You will never eat again, my fine friend.'

Worzel gasped. 'What, never? No sassidges? No more cups o' tea an' slices o' cake? I wouldn't wish that on a danged rook!'

'You wished it upon yourself, though, didn't you, Worzel Gummidge?'

'No I never!' replied the scarecrow stoutly. 'I might be stewpid but I ain't barmy.'

'Oh but you did. You interfered with my plans.'

'Wot plans?'

'My plans for Aunt Sally, of course,' snapped the travelling scarecrow-maker. 'As fine a piece of beechwood as I ever did see. A fine scarecrow she'd make, chopped up and put together again. But you had to come here interfering. You and his high and mightiness the Crowman.'

The mention of the name cheered Worzel up. 'Yes, an' jus' you wait till 'is 'igh an' mightiness comes 'ere a-lookin' for me – you won't 'arf cop it.'

'But he won't, Worzel Gummidge. He doesn't know where to find you.'

'Ho, yes 'e does, clever-britches!' sneered the scarecrow. ''Cos 'e'll look in 'is look-see ball an' there I'll be!'

The travelling scarecrow-maker finished untying Worzel Gummidge and stepped back as the scarecrow flexed his stiff limbs. 'But he hasn't got his crystal ball any more. And without it, your master has no powers.'

'That's what you thinks. The Crowman can do anythink 'e 'as a mind to.' Worzel's voice was a little uncertain, but he was determined to put a brave face on things.

'The Crowman who made *you*, Worzel Gummidge. The Omnipotent Crowman. But the Crowman who made ...' The travelling scarecrow-maker hesitated, as though he was unsure how to phrase what he wanted to say. 'The Crowman who makes the New Zealand scarecrows, has only the powers

86

vested in him by His Omnipotence. And those powers reside in his crystal ball. Without it, he is as straw.'

Worzel Gummidge leapt to his feet. 'An' I's as straw, as well – in fack I *is* of straw, but that won't stop me running off as fast as my twiggy legs'll carry me. An' I'll tell the Crowman, an' Christmas ball or no Christmas ball you'll cop it, jus' you see.'

The travelling scarecrow-maker shrugged and turned his back on the defiant scarecrow. 'Well, Worzel Gummidge, no one's stopping you.'

'I know they ain't.' He pointed at the scarecrow slaves frozen and lifeless at the door. 'Them two ain't, 'cos it ain't dark, and they can't move till then, so nyaah nyaah nyaah!' He thumbed his nose at them. 'An' *you* ain't stoppin' me, 'cos you said you ain't.'

'Then off you go, Worzel Gummidge.'

Worzel Gummidge hesitated, confused by the apparent ease with which his enemy was setting him free. 'I will. I'll be on my way.'

'Good morrow, Worzel Gummidge.'

'An' I wouldn't like to be in your boots when I tell the Crowman you wouldn't give me no breakfuss!' The scarecrow boldly threw open the door. The travelling scarecrow-maker whirled round, seized a blazing log from the brazier and tossed it past Worzel out of the doorway, where a sheet of flame roared up, blocking the way and driving the terrified scarecrow back inside. 'Oo-er! A bon-bon-bon-bon-bon-' he stammered.

The travelling scarecrow-maker dragged the quivering scarecrow back into the room and shoved him roughly on to a bench. 'Exactly. But never fear, Worzel Gummidge – you'll leave soon enough. Only to return.'

'Return? If I gets out o' 'ere wi'out lookin' like a slice o' burnt toast or a baked potatey you'll never see twig nor turnip-ead o' ol' Worzel again,' he replied.

His captor laughed his low, gurgling laugh. 'Oh, but I shall. And not only you, but Aunt Sally too.'

'Aunt Sally? You're dafter nor what I am! What makes you fink Aunt Sally'd come back 'ere, after you was going to chop 'er up to make scarecrow arms an' legs with?'

'Because you'll fetch her, Worzel Gummidge,' said the other softly.

The scarecrow snorted. 'Ho, very likely! "Come on, Aunt Sally – as a special treat ol' Worzel's goin' to take 'ee back to that kind gentleman wot wants to chop your 'ead off."'

'Don't worry, Worzel Gummidge, she'll come.'

'You're barmy!' Worzel insisted. 'I'd 'ave to chop 'er up meself fust!'

The travelling scarecrow-maker's eyes glinted with pleasure. 'You shall, Worzel Gummidge! And carry her back in a sack!' He slithered into one of the gloomiest corners of the room and emerged with an axe and a sack ...

While the children searched, the Crowman tried to distract himself from his troubles by carving a head for a new scarecrow, but it was not going well and he slapped down his scrimshaw-knife in irritation. 'It's no use – I've lost all my concentration.' He unwound his long frame, knees cracking like pistol shots, and began to pace the room, hands clasped in the small of his back, muttering to himself as he paced. 'It must be hidden somewhere – that rogue of a travelling scarecrow-maker can't have carried it off with him – he wouldn't dare. And he won't have destroyed it because he'd destroy himself with it ...' He hauled out his pocket-watch. The time seemed to be crawling past. He shook it, put it to his ear, put it away again. 'Come along, children, come along!' He looked down at the new head staring up at him from the workbench. 'And what are you looking so reproachful about?' he demanded 'Without that crystal ball you're a turnip and nothing more – so make your mind up to it.'

Worzel Gummidge had certainly made his mind up. 'Never

Never never never! You can say what you likes an' do what you likes but I's not goin' to chop up my Aunt Sally an' put 'er in no sack.'

The travelling scarecrow-maker took the outburst quite calmly. 'We shall see, Worzel Gummidge, we shall see. Take the sack.' He held it out to his prisoner.

'Shan't –'.

'There's something in it for you, Worzel Gummidge. A present.'

Worzel wavered. 'A prezzie? For ol' Worzel? No – you's 'avin' me on.'

'Look and see, Worzel Gummidge, look and see.'

'Well ... it *is* my 'ead's birthday, I suppose.'

The travelling scarecrow-maker shook the sack temptingly. Interesting noises came from within. 'Lucky dip, Worzel Gummidge. Try my lucky dip.'

Worzel gave in, plunged his arm deep into the sack, and came up with a parcel wrapped in scraps of old newspaper that smelt as though they had once been used as cat litter. 'Now what in dangnation's this 'ere?' he sniffed.

'Open it ... Happy birthday, Worzel's head!'

Worzel Gummidge tore off the tattered wrapping and gasped in surprise. 'It's another 'ead! Fancy gettin' a new 'ead fer my 'ead's birthday! 'Ere! Now *this* 'ead'll 'ave to 'ave a birthday an' all – so that'll be three birthdays on the same ...' He broke off and peered closely at the carved turnip face. It had the blank, menacing look of one of the travelling scarecrow-maker's zombies. 'My, my, my! That's an ugly 'ead an' no mistake. It could scare cows, could this 'ead, never mind dangnation crows! It's uglier even nor what the one I'se got on already, an' that's sayin' somethin'. Thank'ee very much,' he finished politely.

The travelling scarecrow-maker smiled coldly at Worzel Gummidge's innocence. 'Don't you want to know what kind of a head it is, my fortunate scarecrow?' he asked.

Worzel frowned. 'Let me guess … It's not an 'appy 'ead … an' it ain't a singin' 'ead … an' it ain't a writin' 'ead 'cos it don't 'ave glasses … I don't suppose it's a breakfuss-eatin' 'ead by any chance?' he tried hopefully.

'It's an evil head, Worzel Gummidge!'

'An eelive 'ead!' Worzel looked puzzled. 'I've never come across that word afore. What's eelive, Mister?'

The travelling scarecrow-maker's eyes narrowed to slits. 'Evil's what you'll be when you put it on. Like all my other slave scarecrows.'

'Like all –' He looked up at the ugly zombies either side the door, then down again at the head in his hands. With a chill of recognition he realized that his new head looked exactly like theirs. ''Ere! Now I knows why it's so ugly! You wants to turn me into one o' *them!* So that's what eelive is! No thank'ee, Mister – you keep your eelive 'ead!' He thrust it back at the travelling scarecrow-maker, who folded his arms and refused to take it.

'Put it on, Worzel Gummidge,' he insisted.

The scarecrow shook his head stubbornly. 'Shan't. Shan't shan't shan't!'

'Very well,' hissed his captor. 'You have a choice. You can put your head on now, of your own free will. Or you can come down to my cellar where it's dank and dark, and where you'll find willing helpers to put it on for you.'

'Cellar? You don't get me down in no cellar.'

'Then put it on, Worzel Gummidge, put on your evil head!' Through the grave-like gloom of his filthy hovel the travelling scarecrow-maker advanced threateningly on the scarecrow.

In the bright early-morning sunlight outside, the eager children dragged the Crowman half-stumbling, half-galloping across the meadows and through the woods towards the pond. 'There!' cried Mary urgently as they halted at the water's edge.

The Crowman shaded his eyes and stared. 'Where, child, where?' he wheezed breathlessly.

'*There*! In the middle.' Mickey pointed across the still pond to where a shimmering ball of light flashed and sparkled on the water.

'We couldn't wade in for it,' Mary apologized, ''Cos you told us not to get our feet wet.'

There was sadness in the Crowman's voice. 'Quite right, Mary,' he sighed, 'Quite right.'

'Well,' demanded Mickey, 'Can't you see it?'

He nodded slowly, a wry smile on his old, lined face. 'Yes, I see it –' He lifted Mary easily up and sat her on his shoulders so that she could see from his own height.

'Oh,' she said in a very small voice.

He did the same for Mickey, then lifted him down. 'Oh,' the boy echoed. 'I see. It was just the reflection of the sun –' The children looked crestfallen, but the Crowman still smiled as he patted their heads and turned away from the pond.

'Just the reflection of the early-morning sun, low on the water. But thank you, children. It was a noble try.'

'We'll never find it,' Mary moaned. 'We've looked everywhere.'

'Can we go and play now, Mister Crowman?' asked Mickey.

'Yes ... Off you go.' He waved as the children scuttled off into the woods, then turned away from the pond, and with a heavy heart began to trudge slowly back towards his workshops.

CHAPTER 8

Worzel's First Mission

In the travelling scarecrow-maker's filthy hovel the brave scarecrow finally gave in and unscrewed his ordinary head. He handed it to his jailer, who put the new head into the scarecrow's outstretched hands in its place. 'Take it ... Take your evil head, Worzel Gummidge.' He tossed the old head into the slimy cooking pot. 'And your old head will make a fine broth,' he finished, licking his thin lips. Worzel Gummidge slowly screwed on his new evil head, which at once softened and seemed to take on something of his personality. It was unmistakeably a scarecrow slave's head, and yet the eyes were the mischievous eyes of Worzel Gummidge.

The travelling scarecrow-maker rubbed his bony hands together in gleeful anticipation. 'Well, Worzel Gummidge, my slave scarecrow – and how does your new head feel?'

'Lemme see ...' He tried on a few expressions to see how it felt, leering and sneering, scowling and frowning. 'Same as an orninery 'ead, tell the truth,' he decided. There was something brassy and cocky in his voice that had never been there before, and the pale face of the travelling scarecrow-maker became even paler at the sound. 'Still, it's the thought what counts, ennit?' sniffed Worzel.

The travelling scarecrow-maker was furious. 'What are you grinning at, you stupid scarecrow?' he raged. 'You've nothing to grin at any more – you're evil now, don't you understand that? Evil! Evil!'

Worzel Gummidge stuck his hands on his hips in a challenging gesture. 'Ah, well, that's where you're wrong, Mister. It must be the way Mister Crowman brung me up, see?'

Us scarecrows wot's 'ad life brothe into us can be bad, an' we can be mean, an' we can tell fibs an' we can thieve milk off doorsteps, but we can't be proper eelive – never.'

But his new master was not so easily beaten. 'What a saintly scarecrow you are, Worzel Gummidge,' he sneered. 'But wait until you are properly in my power.'

'Ah, but that'll never 'appen, see.'

'See we shall,' muttered the other to himself. 'See we shall ...' He slithered creepily across the dark, dank room to a shelf where his talisman-scarecrows were displayed and took down a tiny cardboard box covered in mouse droppings and slightly gnawed at one corner. He held it out. 'Another present for you, Worzel Gummidge.'

The scarecrow grabbed it greedily. 'Another prezzie? My, my, my, I *is* a lucky scarecrow today. Wot is it – chocklit?'

'Something you like better than chocolate, Worzel Gummidge,' promised the travelling scarecrow-maker.

Worzel blew some of the mouse droppings off and shook the box. It rattled faintly. 'Well, it can't be a slice o' cake 'cos it's too titchy ...'

'Something you like even better than cake!'

He ripped off the lid, tossed it over his shoulder and squinted down into the box. There, on a bed of oily rags, was a tiny talisman, a miniature figure of his intended. 'Aunt Sally! It's a moggle of my Aunt Sally!' he cried happily.

'A *memento* of Aunt Sally,' the travelling scarecrow-maker corrected him. 'For when she is Aunt Sally no more.'

The scarecrow gave a long-suffering look. 'You keeps chunterin' on about that. Now I've tol'ee I'm not goin' to chop my Aunt Sally up an' put 'er in no sack for you nor nobody else, even if you does give me prezzies – so stop your blatherin'!'

The travelling scarecrow-maker's smile was at its most sinister. 'Take it, Worzel Gummidge, take the talisman!' He lifted it from the box and held it out to the scarecrow. Slowly, as if hypnotized, Worzel reached out to take it. His hand closed round the model, and there was a sudden flash of cold white lightning from the travelling scarecrow-maker's fingers to his own. At once he dropped into a zombie-like trance. The travelling scarecrow-maker lifted his thin arms in triumph. 'Evil be with you in every twig of your body, while ever you hold my talisman! Do you hear your master, Worzel Gummidge?'

He answered in a deep monotone. '*Yes-O-Master.*'

His new master was beside himself with joy. 'Worzel Gummidge, I renounce your name. Henceforth you will be known as slave scarecrow number thirteen. What are you?'

'*Slave-scarecrow-number-eleventy-two-O-Master.*'

'Near enough, near enough.' The travelling scarecrow-maker did a clumsy little jig around the room. 'At last! A slave scarecrow that not only talks but can walk by daylight!' He stopped and addressed his new slave again. 'You are to carry my talisman at all times, slave scarecrow thirteen. Is that clear?'

'*Yes-O-master.*'

The beady little eyes narrowed as he decided to test his new slave straight away. 'And now I have an errand for you. Can you guess what it is?'

'*To-go-find-Aunt-Sally-O-Master.*'

'Excellent! And then ...?' The travelling scarecrow-maker held his breath.

'*Chop-'er-up-an'-put-'er-in-a-sack-O-Master.*'

The talisman had worked! The little sacking-clad figure clapped his hands with glee. 'Splendid! And here's the very chopper –' he scuttled across the room and brought out a rusty but serviceable-looking old axe. 'And here's the very sack.' He produced a sack and dumped the chopper inside it. Worzel Gummidge took them mechanically. 'Bring her to me quickly, slave scarecrow thirteen! Rise!' His slave lumbered awkwardly to his feet as the travelling scarecrow-maker pointed to the open door. 'Go forth! Go forth!' he screeched, and with the sack over his shoulder and a blank expression on his face, Worzel Gummidge plodded away on his dreadful errand.

The children were bored. They wandered through the back streets of Pauahatanui, looking for something to do. Outside the old Majestic cinema they paused to read the poster. 'Return of the Living Dead,' it announced, over a picture of a brain-eater, jaws dripping blood. 'That's supposed to be a good film,' Mickey suggested.

Mary shrugged. 'Forget it, Mickey. They wouldn't let us in.'

'That's right enough. And even if they would we haven't any money left. Come on,' he sighed, turning away.

With their backs to the poster they stopped and gawped – Worzel Gummidge was shambling towards them in his zombie-like trance, eyes blank, grunting to himself like Frankenstein's monster. 'Look at silly old Worzel,' Mary laughed. 'What's he playing at?'

'Monsters!' proclaimed Mickey. 'He's been to see the Return of the Living Dead! Hello, Worzel,' he called. 'Was it as good as Night Of The Blood Beast?'

The scarecrow glowered at them and growled in his throat. '*Grrrr!*'

Mary clapped. 'Oh, that's *very* good! Are you being a living-dead monster, Worzel?'

He growled again, more threateningly. '*Grr-rrr-rrr!*'

'He's not bad, is he?' Mickey pointed to the poster. 'Nearly as good as your brother, Worzel!' The scarecrow's blank eyes went to the poster. With a loud grunt of rage he ripped at a loose corner and tore a strip off.

'Worzel Gummidge!' said Mary rather pompously. 'You've gone too far – as usual. You're nothing but a vandal and if the policeman sees what you've done you'll go to prison!'

But the scarecrow went on clawing at the poster and roaring with rage. '*Grr! Grr! Grr!*' Suddenly, in his clumsy fury, his

Aunt Sally talisman slipped from his awkward fingers and tumbled to the ground. In an instant he was restored to his usual self. 'Go to prison?' he echoed. 'Don't mind if I do – they gives you cups o' tea an' slices o' cake in prison an' I's gone all day without my breakfuss. 'Ere, missus – give us a lick o' that lollipop.'

'Just one – and don't bite it,' warned Mary. She handed her lollipop to Worzel Gummidge and spotted his talisman. 'You've dropped something, Worzel.' She bent to pick it up. 'It's an Aunt Sally doll!'

The scarecrow gave the lollipop a thorough licking, and beamed with delight. 'Ar! Jus' off to see my Aunt Sally, so I am – over at Wicky-wacky-wocky.'

Mary examined the little doll. 'Isn't it lovely!' she cried. A sudden shiver shook her. 'Oo – I've gone all cold!'

'Ar – tis not a playin' doll, see, tis an 'oldin' doll,' Worzel explained, automatically reaching out. She handed it over, glad to be rid of it, and as its power surged through him again his face dropped into a scowl and he returned to his zombie-like trance. '*Grrr. Outa-my-way. I'm-off-to-Wicky-wacky-wocky-for-to-chop-Aunt-Sally's-arms-and-legs-off-an'-put-'em-in-a-sack.*'

'You're horrible! And you can give me back my lollipop!'

The scarecrow slave growled, and took a good bite out of Mary's lollipop. '*Grrr!*' he roared, snatching Mickey's for good measure.

'You give me that back!' Mickey turned on the scarecrow, who raised a clenched fist to drive him back.

'We'll tell the Crowman of you! Come on, Mickey!' and the children raced away, leaving the zombie Worzel Gummidge trudging, growling, toward Waiakikamokau.

'Children, children!' smiled the Crowman as they arrived breathless and gabbling on his doorstep. 'Calm yourselves,

calm yourselves! And do try to talk one at a time, and slowly
... You haven't found my crystal ball?'

Mickey recovered his wind first. 'No,' he gasped. 'It's about
Worzel Gummidge. You know, that man who *says* he's a
scarecrow.'

The Crowman nodded. He tried to remain calm himself,
though he feared the worst. 'Oh yes – I think I know the fellow
you mean. He's quite harmless.'

Mary shook her head furiously. 'No he isn't – he's horrible!'

Her expression alarmed the Crowman. 'You'd better come
in, children.' Inside the house he made tea, brought out cakes
and jam tarts, and listened to their jumbled, garbled story. 'I'm
afraid the man you call Worzel Gummidge is not himself,
children.'

'You're telling me,' said Mickey, helping himself to jam
tarts.

'Tell him about the doll, Mickey,' Mary urged.

The Crowman looked at her sharply. 'What doll?'

'A little model of Aunt Sally,' she continued. '*You* know –
the one in Waiakikamokau museum.'

'Yes,' he said softly, his face drained of colour. 'I know.'

'The funny thing is –' began Mickey through a mouthful of
crumbs.

'The funny thing *is*,' Mary took over, 'when he dropped it he
was nice old Worzel again, but as soon as he picked it up he
was really really nasty.'

'Hm. And he was on his way to Waiakikamokau, you say?'
They nodded together. The Crowman looked grim. He rose
swiftly to his feet and threw on his great cloak. 'Eat up,
children, I have work to do,' he said sternly, and before they
could reply he was gone, striding across the courtyard in the
afternoon sun.

The scarecrow lumbered steadily towards Waiakikamokau.
While he carried his talisman he felt no heaviness in his legs,

and no stray thoughts crept into his turnip brain to distract him or deflect him from his evil errand. He stumped down the road towards the little museum still growling in his throat, not looking right or left, and ignored the local policeman gazing suspiciously in his direction as he marched up the museum steps.

The museum was closed. The angry scarecrow slave tried the door handle, rattling it noisily, but no one came. In his fury he tore down the MUSEUM CLOSED sign, ripped it to shreds, and stamped on the remains. Boiling with frustration he put his shoulder to the door and gave a mighty heave, then hauled the axe out of the sack and began swinging wildly at the woodwork.

That was enough for the policeman. He didn't mind a frustrated visitor having a good bang at the door when they found it unexpectedly closed, but an axe was going a bit far even for Waiakikamokau. He hitched up his belt, strode up the museum steps, and grabbed the scarecrow's arm. 'All right Sunshine! I'll have that,' he announced.

Worzel Gummidge thrust him aside with a roar. 'Don't you struggle with me, matey, or I'll give you something to struggle about,' the burly policeman bellowed, hauling his handcuffs out of his pocket and trying to clamp them on to the flailing scarecrow. They began wrestling, dragging each other down and rolled down the flight of steps, arms locked round one another, to land in a heap on the pavement. In the tussle, the talisman flew out of Worzel Gummidge's hand to land a few feet away ...

At once, he was his old self again. He sat up wearing a broad grin and patted the policeman on the back. 'My, my, my, that fair knocked the stuffin' out o' my stuffin',' he commented in a friendly way. He frowned as the policeman handcuffed his wrists behind his back. ''Ere, what you adoin' of?' he demanded.

'Taking you where you belong. The County jail,' replied the policeman grimly.

There was a coughing rattle as the Crowman's old pick-up wheezed to a halt on the opposite side of the street. 'Oh dear me! What's my – er – odd job man been doing, officer?'

The policeman hauled Worzel Gummidge to his feet. 'Well, Mister Crowman,' he replied. 'You can start with malicious damage, assaulting a police officer, resisting arrest ...'

Worzel blubbered. 'An' now 'e's goin' to put me in prison, Mister Crowman! Don't let 'im tek me away, your graciousness!'

The Crowman took the policeman aside. 'Couldn't we settle this between us, officer?' he suggested quietly. A sudden alarming thought crossed his mind. 'But wait! Malicious damage, you say. Not to any of the museum exhibits, I hope?'

To the Crowman's relief, the policeman shook his head. 'No, I stopped him getting in, or who knows what he'd have smashed up.'

'Hm. On reflection,' the Crowman decided, 'I think a spell in jail might be the safest thing for him.' Ignoring a whimper from Worzel he went on, 'But how are you going to get him there from here?'

The policeman scratched his head. 'Good point, Mister Crowman,' he frowned. 'I hadn't properly worked that out.'

'You can hardly put him over your shoulder ... Supposing I take him to the police station in my truck?' the Crowman suggested helpfully.

'Would you do that?' said the grateful policeman.

'So long as you take the handcuffs off him. Don't want people staring at us.'

The policeman unlocked the handcuffs and spoke sternly to the scarecrow. 'And you behave yourself, or you'll be in worse trouble than you are already.'

'He'll be all right with me, officer,' the Crowman assured him.

Worzel Gummidge nodded meekly. 'Oh, I will, officer. I'll be as good as glod.'

'See that you are! Thanks, Mister Crowman.'

They shook hands, and the Crowman started to lead Worzel towards the truck. 'Come along, Worzel.'

The scarecrow fell in obediently behind his master. 'Yes, Mister Crowman. Whatever you sez, your all-knowingness,' he babbled, glad to be out of the policeman's clutches. As they crossed the quiet little street the talisman exerted its evil influence, and Worzel's eye turned aside and spotted it. 'Oh, just a minute, Mister Crowman. I's forgotten somethink.'

He bent to pick it up, and the Crowman started in alarm. 'Don't touch it!' he cried, but it was too late – the talisman was in Worzel's hand, and the scarecrow was a slave once more. He approached the Crowman menacingly, growling in his throat. 'Now, Worzel, be a sensible scarecrow and come along with me ...'

'*Grrr*!'

The Crowman tried to take the scarecrow's arm to lead him to the truck. 'Worzel – I am the Crowman! I command you to obey me!' he ordered desperately. The scarecrow's only response was to lower his head and butt the Crowman hard in the midriff. He went down, winded, and lay for a moment groaning on the ground. When he looked up again Worzel was nowhere to be seen. Fearing the worst, the Crowman rushed around the side of the museum to the caretaker's entrance, and took the main stairs two at a time towards the exhibition of fairground memorabilia.

He was in time: Worzel Gummidge was not there, and Aunt Sally was still intact in her glass case.

There was a sound from outside, and he rushed to the window to find the scarecrow slave climbing awkwardly up a stolen ladder towards him. 'Worzel!' he called. 'Worzel, listen to me! I have a message from your master, the travelling scarecrow-maker. Aunt Sally is at my house. I am to drive you there. Go and wait in the truck.' It was a last, despairing try, but it worked. The scarecrow slowly descended the ladder, and the Crowman was just about to breathe a sigh of relief and hurry down to join him when he heard a familiar jangling sound.

The tired old horse dragged slowly into view with the cart at its heels, and in response to the travelling scarecrow–maker's beckoning finger Worzel Gummidge turned away from the old pick-up truck and lumbered obediently towards his new master.

The Crowman turned back thoughtfully into the room and approached Aunt Sally's case. 'Come along Aunt Sally,' he murmured, undoing the latch. 'Worzel needs you.'

CHAPTER 9

Aunt Sally Plucks Up Courage

The Crowman drove in silence from Waiakikamokau to Pauahatanui. Perched in the back of his pick-up Aunt Sally waved regally to everyone they passed, for all the world as though she were the Queen of Bohemia on a progress through Transylvania. The Crowman had not made Aunt Sally and had no power over her, but he had known her long enough to know that persuading her to help him save Worzel Gummidge from the evil clutches of the travelling scarecrow-maker was going to be a slow uphill struggle, and long enough indeed to know that the way to her wooden heart was through her stomach.

He gave her a grand tour of inspection round his home and his workshops, and finally settled her down at his long table to a royal tea, whose centrepiece was Worzel Gummidge's head's birthday cake. 'Do help youself, Aunt Sally,' he murmured as she filled her face with chocolate éclairs and jam tarts, Eccles cakes and butterfly buns.

Aunt Sally did not need telling twice, and grabbed a Battenburg with both hands. 'Ho I will, your Honour, and thanks ever so much for hasking me hout to tea,' she spluttered through a mouthful of crumbs.

'My pleasure,' said the Crowman.

'Hi did 'ave a number of hengagements,' she lied grandly, 'but my social seckyteckytry will 'ave cancelled them by now, so I can stop till Hi've 'ad sufficience.' She paused for breath, and a genteel hiccup escaped from her rosebud-painted mouth. 'Pardon.'

'A little bread and butter, Aunt Sally?' enquired her host, for the bread and butter had not been touched. He took a slice himself, and nibbled a crustless corner.

Aunt Sally shook her head. 'Never touch it, your 'ighness. It's bad for my pretty face, you know,' she declared. ''Specially when there's cake going,' and she grabbed a long knife and lunged clumsily towards the birthday cake.

The Crowman got there first and took away the knife. 'Ah, now that I'm afraid is not for you, Aunt Sally. The butterfly buns, cream gâteaux, and jam tarts by all means – but that happens to be Worzel's head's birthday cake.'

She frowned and drummed her fingers on the table in frustration. 'Ho, it's one of 'is birthdays, his it? Hi wish I'd 'ad a note in my diary – I would have sent 'im 'alf a brick, gift-wrapped. Even though he *didn't* invite me to his party, the 'alf-witted, 'orrible 'aystack.'

Gently steering the conversation to what he really wanted to discuss, the Crowman continued. 'Were I giving Worzel a birthday party, Aunt Sally, you'd be the first guest on his list, as you perfectly well know. But he's *not* here for his birthday and that's what I want to talk to you about.'

'Don't tell me, let me guess. Your Honour wants to give *me* a birthday party, bein' as 'ow I'm more in the social swim?' she smirked. 'You're so kind. Let me see, hif memory serves me right, I shall be nineteen and a 'arf on Febtember the thirty-twoth.'

The Crowman sighed. It *was* going to be an uphill struggle! 'I have not brought you here to talk about birthday parties, Aunt Sally. Or simply to feed your face. Worzel Gummidge is in danger.'

She shrugged carelessly. 'Oh yes? Could you pass me three or four of them jam tarts, please?'

'He's been captured by the Travelling Scarecrow-Maker,' the Crowman went on, sliding a plate piled high with jam tarts towards her.

Aunt Sally shuddered. 'Oo – 'Orrible man! Kindly change

the subjick whilst we're partaking hof our tea, Mister Crowman – *hif* you please.' The subject of the horrible man didn't seem to put her off her tea, though, and as the Crowman went on she began popping in jam tarts and munching them whole.

'You don't seem to understand, Aunt Sally. Unless we do something, Worzel could well end his days as one of that scoundrel's slave scarecrows.'

''E won't mind,' she said between tarts. ''E quite likes fetching and carrying.'

A note of anger began to creep into the Crowman's voice. 'For you, Aunt Sally. For nobody else – not even me. And who's going to fetch and carry for you if Worzel isn't here?'

She stopped gorging just long enough to flutter her eyelashes and purse her lips at her host. 'Couldn't your Honour make another scarecrow, just for pretty me?' she simpered. 'A more 'andsome one this time, one that looks like a fillum star, with a lickle moustache and black wavy hair and gleaming white –'

The Crowman snapped. 'Aunt Sally! Do you ever think of anyone but yourself? Worzel has to be saved!'

She sat up very straight, looked directly in front of her and sank her teeth into another éclair, ignoring the cream that oozed out across her rouged cheeks. 'Just as your Honour says,' she spluttered squelchily. 'But what's it got to do with me?'

'You, Aunt Sally, are the one who's going to do it.'

Aunt Sally's eyebrows quivered, and her voice rose to a bat-like squeak. 'Me? Go back to the Travelling Scarecrow-Maker's 'ouse after he tried to chop me up like a bundle of firewood? Heggscuse me for making so bold, but your Honour must be off his Honour's trolley.'

'It's a brave thing to ask of you, Aunt Sally, but it's the only way,' the Crowman insisted.

'Begging your parding,' she replied stiffly, 'but he's *your* scarecrow.'

The Crowman suddenly looked very old and very tired. 'I know that, but without my crystal ball my powers are weak. If I set foot in that house of evil I should be destroyed and all my scarecrows with me.'

Aunt Sally wasn't convinced. 'But what about pretty me? 'E'd saw my 'ead off as soon as look at me.'

'I've thought of that, Aunt Sally. You must go in disguise.'

For a moment the idea appealed to Aunt Sally's vanity. 'I could go as the Queen of Bo'emia, else a Grand Duchess ...' She hesitated, then shook her head firmly and reached for a raspberry meringue. 'No, but he'd still reggernise me, 'cos of my beautiful eyes and ruby red lips. The whole idea's prepospospospos.'

'I'm appealing to you, Aunt Sally,' he begged. 'Not for my sake, but for Worzel's.'

She put on a prim, butter-wouldn't-melt expression. 'But Worzel means nothink to me, your Honour.'

'Worzel loves you.'

Aunt Sally shrugged. 'More fool 'im.'

'Don't you love him back?' the Crowman implored her. 'Not even a little?'

Aunt Sally looked extremely high-and-mighty. 'Hi might do. Hi might not. Hit would never do for him to get big-'eaded.'

The Crowman sighed wearily. He seemed to be getting nowhere. 'You'd miss Worzel more than you know, Aunt Sally. He rescued you from the travelling scarecrow-maker's clutches – now it's your turn to rescue him.'

'Couldn't I 'ave just a titchy slice of Worzel's birthday cake, your Honour?' she pouted.

'Aunt Sally,' the Crowman roared in frustration. 'For the last time – *will you do it*?'

She considered the matter, her head cocked on one side. The idea of a disguise still appealed to her vanity. 'Is it a pretty disguise?' she asked at last. The Crowman smiled, knowing that he'd won.

In the sunlit courtyard outside the Crowman's workshop the children were playing football beside the old millpond. They glanced up as the workshop door opened and a curious-looking individual with a strong resemblance to Charlie Chaplin came out, with a briefcase bearing the legend 'Acme Insurance', and a little black moustache.

'Good luck,' said the Crowman solemnly, patting the insurance salesman on the shoulder. Mickey and Mary watched him cross the courtyard with a stiff-legged walk that seemed somehow familiar to them, then shrugged and went back to their game as he disappeared down the green lane.

There was a smell of stale cabbage and mutton fat in the travelling scarecrow-maker's filthy hovel, and a haze of stinging smoke from the rickety brazier. Worzel Gummidge's beady eyes watered as his new master tied the Aunt Sally talisman round his neck with a length of old garden twine. 'Just to ensure that you don't let go of it again. That would never do, would it, slave scarecrow number thirteen?'

The scarecrow's voice was a harsh monotone. '*No-O-Master.*'

The travelling scarecrow-maker straightened up and looked sourly down on his latest slave. 'Now to your tasks for the day,' he announced. 'You'll scrub the floor and wash the dishes and whitewash the cellar and make my tea and clean my boots. Then at nightfall you'll accompany slave scarecrows numbers three, seven and nine back to that museum, and this time you will return with Aunt Sally – is that understood?' He picked up a saw and ran his bony finger lovingly along the teeth.

'*Yes-O-Master,*' replied Worzel Gummidge dully.

'And should you fail?' asked his captor in his sinister, silky voice.

106

'*I'll-be-chucked-on-the-bonfire.*'

The travelling scarecrow-maker was satisfied. 'So you shall,' he agreed. 'Now get to work,' Worzel Gummidge lurched to his feet and set out on his long day's labours.

Aunt Sally was scared. Her disguise was not at all what she had had in mind – an insurance salesman, indeed! – and there was a dark, brooding atmosphere hanging over the path through the woods that made her sharp little eyes dart nervously from side to side. If she had seen the scarecrow slaves behind the bushes at every turn she might not have been able to go on at all, but the travelling scarecrow-maker had hidden them all well, and soon she emerged into the damp clearing where no birds sang, and approached the filthy hovel.

She tiptoed towards the door, gulping with fright. For a moment she froze, and half-turned away, but the thought of what the Crowman would say drove her on. She lifted a trembling hand to the knocker – let it drop – lifted it again – and finally screwed up her courage enough for a timid knock. The travelling scarecrow-maker opened the door a crack and peered suspiciously out at her. 'What do you want?' he barked.

Aunt Sally raised her bowler hat. 'Heggscuse me, but 'ave you hever thought of 'avin' your 'ovel hinsured' she quavered. 'P'raps hi could show you some –' The door slammed in her face. 'Literiteriterure,' she tailed off weakly. She turned her back on the hovel and scuttled away, stiff-legged, through the wood. Her relief at being away from that dreadful place completely elbowed aside any feelings she might have had about failing to rescue Worzel Gummidge.

The travelling scarecrow-maker rubbed a clearish patch on a filthy window with his sacking sleeve and frowned in thought as he watched the insurance salesman disappear. Was there something familiar about that figure? he wondered. He decided not, and put the thought out of his mind.

*

An hour later, while Worzel Gummidge was up to his elbows in the chipped stone sink, washing a mountain of greasy, encrusted crockery in luke-warm water, there was another knock at the door. The travelling scarecrow-maker glanced up from his stolen library book and scowled. 'Answer the door, slave scarecrow number thirteen,' he ordered. The words penetrated Worzel Gummidge's turnip brain, but under the power of the talisman he had become slow and clumsy, and set out so ponderously across the room that the travelling scarecrow-maker impatiently waved him back to the sink. 'Oh, you're so slow – I'll answer it myself ... yes, yes, coming!' he called sharply as the knocking was repeated.

He threw open the creaking door and blinked in surprise. On the doorstep stood a bearded figure in rimless glasses with a peaked cap boldly labelled 'GAS'. 'Yes?' the travelling scarecrow-maker snarled.

'Heggscuse me for hinterrupting you at teatime,' said Aunt Sally through the false beard. 'But I 'ave come to cut off your gas.'

The travelling scarecrow-maker frowned. 'I don't have gas,' he said.

Aunt Sally nodded seriously. 'That must hexplain why you 'aven't paid your bill. Hif you like, Hi could put some gas in for you. Hit's very reasonalalalable,' she offered.

'I don't need gas. My brazier is good enough for me.'

Aunt Sally tried hard. 'Hi could fetch you a sample of gas hif you'd like to try it. Hit gets much 'otter than common coal, you know.'

The travelling scarecrow-maker lost his patience. 'Go away!' he barked, slamming the door. As Aunt Sally scampered stiff-leggedly away across the yard he again watched thoughtfully through the smeared window. He decided to act, and turned to the scarecrow slave, still plodding through the pile of greasy plates. 'Leave the washing up, slave scarecrow number thirteen, and come to me,' he ordered. 'Quicker!' he snapped as Worzel Gummidge stumped heavily across the room. 'I have an errand for you.'

'*I-will-obey-O-Master.*'

The travelling scarecrow-maker sneered. 'You'd better! I want you to follow that so-called gas inspector and see where he goes. Don't follow him indoors, mind! Then come back and tell me what you've seen.'

'*Yes-O-Master!*' said Worzel dully.

His captor pushed him roughly to the door. 'Hurry then, or you'll lose him!' Worzel Gummidge stumbled out, blinking in the bright daylight. 'Quickly!' snapped his new master, as Worzel started to move at an awkward, zombie-ish jog-trot after Aunt Sally.

She hated the woods, and pushed on through them as fast as her stiff little legs would carry her, never pausing, even when she thought she heard twigs crack on the path behind her, never looking to right or left, even when she was sure there were eyes following her flight, until she emerged into the sweet-smelling air of the meadows beyond. There she sat for a moment on a convenient bench to recover her breath. 'Stupid Worzel!' she complained. 'Why can't he rescue himself, I should like to know? It'd serve him right if I abanbanban-doned 'im to 'is evil fate...'

Having got her breath back she rose from her bench and walked on more slowly towards the Crowman's house, quite unaware of the slave scarecrow at her heels...

Even in the safety of the Crowman's house she was tearful and fearful, and had to chomp furiously on a nutty piece of Dundee cake to calm herself. The Crowman poured a cup of tea and tut-tutted sympathetically as she told her tale. 'It's no use, Mister Crowman, sir, I'm frykkened to go back there any more,' she snivelled. 'Anyway, what's the point? 'E won't let me into 'is 'ovel and even hif 'e did, 'e'd only saw my 'ead off. Is there any more cake?'

'Of course there is, Aunt Sally,' said the Crowman soothingly. 'Now don't take on so. You're my only hope, so you musn't weaken.'

Aunt Sally sniffled. 'I'd better 'ave a bigger slice o' cake for my strength then.'

The Crowman stood up and started to pace the room, stroking his long chin with his thumb. 'We've just been going about it the wrong way, that's all. Now let me think...'

Almost as much afraid of what the Crowman's next brainwave might be as of the travelling scarecrow-maker himself, Aunt Sally guzzled another slice of cake, wide-eyed and shivering.

The travelling scarecrow-maker was delighted when Worzel returned with his news. 'To the Crowman's house, you say?' he hissed. 'Are you sure?'

Worzel nodded robotically. '*Yes-O-Master.*'

'As I thought, as I thought.' The travelling scarecrow-maker started to pace his room in the same slow manner as the Crowman, furiously thinking what his next move might be.

The simplest solution to a problem is generally the best, though it is also sometimes the hardest to think of. When he had thought of his brilliant solution and given Aunt Sally her orders the Crowman shook his head in annoyance that it had taken him so long. Licking the tip of a pencil he began to make notes on an old piece of parchment.

There was a crash that made him jump and snap the point of his pencil. He strode to the window and stared out at the children, kicking their football against his door. 'Can't you children go and play somewhere else?' he asked, rather sharply. 'I'm very busy with a great deal on my mind today.'

'Sorry, Mister Crowman,' they chorused.

He turned back into the room, muttering to himself. 'Blessed children! How can a body concentrate!'

A muffled voice came from behind a lacquered Japanese screen. 'Thu woo bru soo poo poo poo.'

'What's that, Aunt Sally?' he asked, sharpening his pencil again to a fine point.

Aunt Sally's head popped up over the screen, her mouth splodged with jam. 'Sorry, your Honour, I was swallerin' a jam tart,' she gulped. 'Hi said they wasn't brung up proper, the same as what Hi was.'

He waggled a hand at her. 'Yes, well, get on with your changing, Aunt Sally. We've got no time to lose.' Her head promptly popped out of sight again behind the screen, and he carried on his notes where he had left off, sucking the end of his pencil thoughtfully from time to time. 'Now where was I ... It's vital that we get your speech to the travelling scarecrow-maker absolutely right this time.' His pacing took him to the still-open window just at the moment when a misdirected kick sent the football through it, catching him fair and square on the back of the head. He threw down his pencil in irritation and glared out at the children.

'Can we have our ball back, please, Mister Crowman?' called Mickey nervously.

The Crowman was breathing hard to control his wrath. 'This is the very last time. If I see this football again I shall confiscate it. Now be off with you!' He threw the ball back and slammed the window noisily shut.

Mary breathed a sigh of relief. 'Yes, Mister Crowman.' She looked at Mickey. 'Come on. He really means it this time.'

'All right.' Mickey turned his back on the house and gave the football an aimless boot. It lifted high in the air in a tight arc, and came down with a little splash in the weed-covered millpond. They ran to the low wall and peered into the cool green depths. 'Do you think the Crowman'll fish it out for us?' asked Mickey without much hope in his voice.

Mary shook her head. 'Somehow I don't think he would.'

There was nothing to be seen but a thick tangle of green

water weed, and wherever the ball was, it was beyond the reach of their short arms. 'Come on, let's get our shrimping nets,' Mickey suggested, and they scampered off together to fetch them.

The Crowman was too wrapped up in his work to notice their departure. Scribbling furiously, he muttered to himself, 'Yes, yes, that should work the trick, if anything can. I don't know why I didn't think of this sooner, Aunt Sally. I must have lost my brains as well as my crystal ball.'

'So long as hit's understood,' came Aunt Sally's voice from behind the screen, 'that this is my very last hattempt, your Honour. Hafter this, Worzel Gummidge can stew in 'is own straw.'

'Come along, Aunt Sally, don't be so hard.'

Her head popped up, a pert expression on her jammy face. 'That's as may be, Mister Crowman, but if Worzel loses 'is 'ead you can always make 'im another one. You can even make an 'ole Worzel hif your Honour as a mind to – but 'oo's going to make a new Aunt Sally? Hi'm unikew,' she declared proudly.

'No one's going to lose their head, Aunt Sally,' he reassured her, though he touched wood as he spoke. 'Now come out and let's have a look at you.' From behind the screen Aunt Sally emerged, in her best disguise yet – as a bent old woman with a gnarled stick and a tattered shawl. Beaming with satisfaction the Crowman picked up an artist's palette and moved towards her to do her make-up. 'Excellent, excellent! You should have been an actress, Aunt Sally,' he declared.

Her eyes widened. 'Ho, Hi was! Hi was in 'Amlet and Juliet – didn't your Honour know?'

He smiled indulgently. 'It must have slipped my mind … Now let's give you a few wrinkles, Aunt Sally, and then you must learn your lines.'

The travelling scarecrow-maker's plans were progressing as rapidly as his opponent's. With Worzel Gummidge lumbering at his heels the grey figure slithered out into his yard. 'Now to prepare for our visitor,' he hissed, rubbing his sacking-mittened palms together. 'To the woodshed, slave scarecrow number thirteen.'

'*Yes-O-Master.*' The scarecrow stumped obediently across the yard to the woodshed, wrenched open the door, lurched inside and pulled the door shut behind him.

His new master stamped angrily. 'Not *in* the woodshed, you snivelling half-wit. I want you to bring in some logs. We are going to make a big, big fire.'

Worzel Gummidge emerged from the woodshed blinking and covered in cobwebs. '*Yes-O-Master.*' He picked up a huge log and staggered towards the travelling scarecrow-maker's hovel.

Just as Mary and Mickey galloped breathlessly back into the Crowman's courtyard and began fishing in the millpond with their shrimping nets, the workshop door creaked open and Aunt Sally emerged in her latest disguise, bent almost double and carrying over her arm a basket of new-laid eggs. The children stared at her: even in disguise she could not conceal her stiff-legged, swaying walk. She beamed at them. 'Good afternoon, kiddiwinks,' she croaked.

'Good afternoon, Ma'am,' they chorused politely.

'Har you 'aving a nice play? That's the idea!' she cackled, thoroughly enjoying her new character for the moment, and hobbled on her way.

They watched her with thoughtful frowns. 'The Crowman's had a lot of visitors today,' said Mary.

Mickey nodded. 'Yes. Isn't it funny how they all walk the same?' he answered, plunging his net into the millpond.

'Mm, I noticed that … Mickey, do you know who I think it is?'

But the boy gave an excited shout and began hauling up his net. 'Just a minute, I think I've got our ball.' Mary ran over to

113

lend a hand, but their catch was only an old boot. The Crowman's strange stream of visitors forgotten, they carried on fishing.

CHAPTER 10

The Traveller Unmasked

The travelling scarecrow-maker cackled happily as Worzel Gummidge piled up fresh logs on to the bonfire. 'That will do, I think, slave scarecrow number thirteen. Nothing like a nice fire to welcome our visitor.'

Worzel croaked his agreement. '*Oo-ar-O-Master-our-visitor-should-burn-werry-nicely-on-that-there-fire.*'

The other turned and looked at him sharply. 'Did I ask you to speak?' he hissed.

'*No-O-master, 'umbly-sorry-O-Master,*' the scarecrow grovelled.

'Then keep your turnip tongue in your turnip head,' snapped the travelling scarecrow-maker. He gave a low chuckle, and scuttled indoors to fetch a blazing brand from the brazier. 'Besides, the fire isn't for our visitor. Beechwood is far too valuable to burn. The fire, slave scarecrow number thirteen – just in case anything goes wrong with my little plan – is for you!' and he thrust the flame towards the terrified scarecrow and drove him indoors.

He did not have long to wait. Standing with his flat nose pressed to the dripping window pane he soon caught sight of the little old lady hobbling out from the shadow of the trees, and gave a soft chuckle. 'Won't you walk in to my parlour, said the spider to the fly ...' he murmured.

As Aunt Sally approached the filthy hovel for the third time her lips moved soundlessly in a heartfelt prayer. 'Please let 'im be out!' she whispered as she knocked with her gnarled stick.

The travelling scarecrow-maker beckoned Worzel to him.

'Admit our visitor, slave scarecrow number thirteen. Then lock the door!' he added viciously.

The zombie-like figure of Worzel Gummidge opened the door. Aunt Sally pretended not to recognize him. 'Good afternoon,' she said faintly. 'I spec you're the butler.'

Worzel bowed. '*That's-right-modom.*'

Shocked by his robot-like voice she stopped pretending. 'What you talking like that for?' she demanded.

'*Never-you-mind-modom-what-can-I-do-for-you?*'

'Is your master at 'ome?' she asked, trying to look composed.

The scarecrow nodded. '*Yes-'e-is-'e-sez-fer-you-to-come-in.*'

He held the door open, and a trembling Aunt Sally hobbled over the threshhold. Behind her, the door crashed shut and the bolts were slammed home. The travelling scarecrow-maker came forward, cringing and wringing his hands, to welcome his guest. 'Good afternoon, madame. Welcome to my humble residence. And what can I do for you?'

Aunt Sally cleared her throat nervously. 'Are you –' Her voice came out a pitch too high. She coughed daintily and tried again. 'Are you the Travelling Scarecrow-Maker?'

He smiled his greasy smile and spread his hands. 'For my sins, madame, for my sins.'

'Hi ham Mrs Handerson,' announced Aunt Sally, reciting the lines that the Crowman had written for her. 'A 'umble small'older from Wicky-wacky-wocky. Hi was wondering hif you could make me a scarecrow.'

The travelling scarecrow-maker seemed to be delighted. 'I *do* make scarecrows, as you can see, madame. Poor things, but mine own.' He turned sharply to Worzel Gummidge 'Why are you keeping our lady guest standing? Fetch her a chair, then help her to some tea,' he ordered. As he turned back again to Aunt Sally his voice became silky and smarmy once more. 'You will stay to tea, madame?'

Aunt Sally's eyes fell greedily on a plate of cakes and Danish

116

pastries that the clever travelling scarecrow-maker had placed temptingly on a shaky little table, and, as he had calculated, her greed overcame her fear. 'Hi don't mind hif I do, while we talks business.' As Worzel Gummidge shuffled up with her chair she pointed at the cakes. 'I'll 'ave one o' them an' two o' them an' three o' them … To begin with,' she decided.

'*Yes-O-Modom*,' droned the scarecrow. He fetched the plate of cakes and watched enviously as Aunt Sally began to fill her face.

Aunt Sally was impressed. 'My, my, you 'ave got 'im well-trained, 'aven't you, Mister Travelling Scarecrow-Maker?'

'All my staff are well-trained, madame – the better to receive our *visitors* …' he said with a chilling hiss. 'Now, as to madame's requirements – you're troubled by rooks, are you?'

'Somethink chronic,' she agreed.

'When I have made *you* a scarecrow, madame, you will be troubled no more.' There was a subtle double meaning in his words that Aunt Sally completely missed. 'You'll find my charges reasonable.'

The Crowman had guessed that the conversation might turn to money, and had allowed for it in the script he had written. 'Ah, well,' Aunt Sally parrotted, 'Bein' of 'umble circumspectances – even more 'umble than what yours is – Hi don't actually 'ave any money. But Hi could pay you hin heggs.' She showed him her basket of fresh eggs.

The travelling scarecrow-maker rubbed his hands in anticipation. 'That would be most satisfactory,' he declared. 'I like an egg for my tea when the day's work is done. Now,' he gestured at the motionless scarecrows around the room, and at the spare, half-carved heads and not-quite-finished arms and legs that lay stacked up in corners. 'What kind of scarecrow would madame like? Look around you and you'll see some samples of my work.'

Helping herself with both hands to more cakes, Aunt Sally pretended to examine the zombie scarecrows and the shabby

117

fragments. 'Ooh, they're a hugly lot, hain't they? They'd scare me, never mind the rooks.' She looked Worzel Gummidge up and down as if she was seeing him for the very first time. ''Owever, this one hain't 'alf bad.'

'*Thank-you-O-Modom*,' droned Worzel, to the travelling scarecrow-maker's fury.

'Silence!' he snarled, raising a threatening fist to his scarecrow slave. He turned to Aunt Sally and gushed. 'But this is my servant, madame. As you can see, he walks and talks.'

She dismissed his objections with an airy wave of her hand. 'That don't matter – you can knock a bit off the price in heggs for 'im bein' a bit shop-soiled. So hif you'll just wrap 'im hup in a bit o' brown paper Hi'll polish hoff these cakes and be hon my way.'

The travelling scarecrow-maker shook his head. 'I couldn't allow it, madame. Not until I have made *you* a scarecrow,' he repeated.

Aunt Sally was starting to get uneasy, and was eager to be off. 'But Hi don't need one making. Hi've told you – Hi'll take this ready-made one.'

Her host loomed over her and reached a bony forefinger to touch her arm. 'But the one I make will be a special scarecrow, madame. With legs and arms of the finest *beechwood*!'

'Beechwood?' she quavered.

'Quite so. And as finely carved a head as you ever did see. Wouldn't you like that … *Aunt Sally*!' he finished, whipping off her grey wig and granny glasses triumphantly.

In the courtyard outside the Crowman's house Mickey had grown bored with sloshing about in the murkey depths, and sat on the cobbles with his back to the cool stone wall of the millpond, soaking up the afternoon sun, while Mary fished for footballs. 'I still can't see it, Mickey,' she sighed. 'It must have sunk.'

'Footballs don't sink, stupid,' he pointed out scornfully. 'It's hidden under all that pond weed.'

She leaned over the wall and plunged her net in again. 'I'm going to have one more dip,' she decided, 'And then I'm going home for my tea.' She tottered on the brink as the net met something heavy, then gave a little squeak that brought Mickey to his feet. 'Mickey! I think I've got it!'

'Careful! Don't let it slip!' With enormous care they hauled the dripping shrimping net out of the millpond and laid it on the ground. Plunging both hands into the tangled mess of pond weed, Mary gasped as she brought out, not their football, but a glowing crystal globe, swirling with the grey mists of time and space. For a moment they were silent with wonder, then looked at one another in amazement and rushed off yelling to find their friend. 'Mister Crowman! Mister Crowman!'

He was in his workshop, hunched over his bench, and far from pleased to see the children rushing in with a suspicious-looking bulge under Mickey's jacket. 'Hello, Mister Crowman,' cried Mary breathlessly, 'Look what we've got!'

The Crowman raised a finger. 'What have I told you children about playing with that wretched football outside my ...' he began, but as Mickey produced the crystal ball a slow smile of infinite relief spread across his lined and weary features. 'Bless my soul!' he breathed happily. 'Bless my soul!'

Moments later, crouched over the crystal ball in the privacy of his study, the Crowman watched events unfolding and pursed his lips. 'Worse than I thought!' he decided. 'This means a personal visit.'

In the gloomy atmosphere of the travelling scarecrow-maker's filthy hovel Aunt Sally was begging for mercy. 'Oh please, Mister Travelling Scarecrow-Maker, don't 'urt me!' She fell on her knees at his sacking-wrapped feet, knocking over the cakestand and scattering the few remaining cakes in the dirt. 'I'm too pretty to be 'urt!'

The travelling scarecrow-maker was unmoved by her pleas, though he enjoyed seeing her grovelling. 'Fetch me the saw, slave scarecrow number thirteen,' he ordered coldly, and Worzel Gummidge lumbered off without a word.

'Don't listen to him, Worzel!' she begged. 'Aren't you going to 'elp me? I thought you was my sweetheart!'

The scarecrow ignored her, waggling the blade of the rusty saw as he brought it towards his master. '*Shall-I-saw-'er-'ead-off-O-Master*?' he suggested.

Aunt Sally squeaked with terror. 'Oh, Worzel, you wouldn't! Not to your Aunt Sally!'

A nasty thought crawled into the travelling scarecrow-maker's mind. 'Why shouldn't he, my pretty one?' he murmured.

''Cos 'e loves me,' she wailed. ''E even wants to marry me! Look – 'e even wears a likkle moggle of me round 'is hugly neck!' She pointed at the talisman the travelling scarecrow-maker had tied round Worzel Gummidge's neck a few hours earlier.

The travelling scarecrow-maker's eyes narrowed with mischief. 'Do you like my little doll, Aunt Sally?' he asked. As she nodded he muttered to himself, rubbing his hands, 'That gives me an idea for some sport!' He untied the doll. 'Then you shall have it!'

Released from the hateful influence of the talisman Worzel Gummidge blinked twice and gazed round the room as though he had forgotten where he was. 'Oh, 'ello, Aunt Sally – wot are *you* a-doin' of?' he asked, his normal self once more.

'I've come to take you 'ome, Worzel,' she answered boldly. She faced the travelling scarecrow-maker with a defiant stare. ''Cos now 'e's stopped bein' funny we're two against one – so 'and over my lickle doll an' we'll be hoff!'

The scarecrow gasped as she held out her hand for the talisman. 'Don't take it, Aunt Sally!' he croaked in alarm, lunging forward to stop her.

He was too slow.

The travelling scarecrow-maker slipped the talisman round Aunt Sally's slender neck and cackled with delight. 'There! Do you like your little doll – *slave scarecrow number fourteen*?'

Her voice came out in a high-pitched monotonous drone. '*Yes-O-Master-thank-you-very-much-O-Master.*'

'Oh, Aunt Sally!' cried the dismayed scarecrow. 'Don't be 'is slave scarecrow number fourteen! Let me be your slave number eleventy an' take you away from 'ere.'

The travelling scarecrow-maker sneered at him. He had served his purpose as bait for beechwood and now he was no further use. 'Your turnip head talks too much. What shall we do with him, slave scarecrow number fourteen?'

'*Chuck-'im-on-the-bonfire-O-Master*,' his new slave answered blankly.

'Exactly!'

Worzel Gummidge threw himself gibbering at the dull-eyed doll's dainty feet, and clasped his twiggy fingers as if in prayer. 'No! Spare me! Don't let me be chucked on the bon-bon-bon-bon- arter all I've done for 'ee, Aunt Sally! Please!' he moaned, as the travelling scarecrow-maker cackled fiendishly.

In only a few minutes Worzel Gummidge was strapped to a rough scarecrow pole and planted firmly in the middle of the bonfire he had himself built earlier in the afternoon. He watched miserably as the zombie-like figure of Aunt Sally piled up branches around his feet. 'Oh, Aunt Sally, I never thought you'd do this to pore ol' Worzel, never in a thousy-trillion years,' he moaned.

The travelling scarecrow-maker cut short his babbling with a wave of his hand. 'That will do, slave scarecrow number fourteen ... Now, slave scarecrow number thirteen, have you a last request?' he asked.

'Yes, I 'ave,' said Worzel bravely. He gazed adoringly at Aunt Sally. 'Will you marry me, Aunt Sally?' he begged.

She scoffed at him. '*Har-har-har-O-slave-scarecrow.*'

'Not to her, nincompoop,' snapped the travelling scarecrow-maker irritably. 'To me! What is your last request?'

Even in his miserable state Worzel's heart was in the right place. 'My last request?' he echoed forlornly. 'It's fer you to do what you likes with me, but to let my Aunt Sally go, an' let 'er find an 'andsome prince else a duke an' marry 'im an' live in a castle with servants to fetch 'er all the cakes and jellies an' limmonade she can swoller – an' for 'er to live 'appily ever after.'

His captor cackled with spiteful laughter. 'Last request not granted!'

'*Shall-I-light-the-bonfire-O-Master?*' asked Aunt Sally.

The travelling scarecrow-maker shook his head. 'All in good time, slave scarecrow number fourteen. We'll wait till sundown, when all my slave scarecrows come to life. Let them gather around and see what's the penalty for disobedience!' Over the trees, the sun was rapidly setting. In only a few more minutes it would be dark. Worzel Gummidge sagged on his scarecrow pole as the travelling scarecrow-maker squelched through the mud and slithered into his filthy hovel with the obedient Aunt Sally at his heels.

As the sun sank behind the trees the scarecrow slaves watching the path through the woods began to stir and sway. In an ominous grey line they shuffled past Worzel through the gloom and made their way into the travelling scarecrow-maker's hovel. When the last one was out of sight there was a rustle of leaves at the woods' edge and the Crowman emerged, grim-faced, and hurried to untie the scarecrow. 'Thank goodness you's come Mister Crowman, sir – I knowed you would,' he whispered happily. 'But don't bother about ol' Worzel, your untieingness – 'e's got Aunt Sally.'

But the Crowman had a plan. 'One thing at a time, Worzel. Quickly now – I need your help.' He beckoned, and led the way to where a half-completed scarecrow lay. 'That'll do. Give me a hand.' Working swiftly and silently they strapped the scarecrow to the pole in the bonfire, clapped Worzel's hat on its head, then stepped back to examine the effect. In the dusk it would do...

There was a sound from the hovel. The Crowman pushed Worzel Gummidge out of sight behind a low, tumbledown wall, and they watched in breathless silence as the door opened. The travelling scarecrow-maker emerged with Aunt Sally at his heels, carrying a blazing torch, and after them the monstrous shapes of the scarecrow slaves shuffled out into the yard and gathered in a circle round the bonfire.

The travelling scarecrow-maker looked around with satisfaction. 'Time, I think, my pretty one ...' he nodded to Aunt Sally. 'Light the bonfire!' Without even a glance at the scarecrow on the pole she put her torch to the brushwood and stepped back as the flames crackled up into the grey dusk. The travelling scarecrow-maker cackled with glee as the scarecrow began to burn.

The Crowman stepped forward with a hesitant Worzel Gummidge at his heels. 'Yes,' he declared, 'we *shall* need a bonfire!'

The travelling scarecrow-maker staggered back in astonishment. 'You!' he gasped. He spotted the trembling Worzel, and turned to the figure on the pole. 'You have tricked me! But for the last time!' he spat. He addressed the zombie band. 'Seize them!'

'Not so fast!' The Crowman moved like a black shadow to Aunt Sally's side, snatched the talisman from her neck and hurled it into the flames. Dense clouds of sulphurous smoke billowed up, and the travelling scarecrow-maker and his scarecrow slaves shrank back in terror before the powerful figure. 'I am the Crowman!' he roared. 'By all the elements, let this be a cleansing fire!' and he hurled on to the fire a curious powder. The smoke died away, and the flames changed colour, shimmering around the rainbow from red to orange to yellow to green to blue to indigo to violet and back again to red. The Crowman slowly raised his arm and pointed at the cowering zombies. 'I command you – march into the flames!'

His power was strong enough. One by one, as blank-faced as ever, the scarecrow slaves shuffled slowly forward and were consumed by the healing flames. The travelling scarecrow-maker's voice was low. 'Do your worst, Master. There will be more,' he promised.

The Crowman sighed. 'I know that. More slave scarecrows. More evil. I shall never stop fighting it. Or you.'

As the procession of scarecrow slaves continued to march blindly into the flames, Worzel Gummidge crossed quickly to his intended. 'Is you all right now, Aunt Sally?' he asked tenderly.

'Yes thank you, Worzel,' she nodded. 'Are you?'

He looked unhappily at the flickering flames. 'I shall be as soon as we gets away from this bon-bon-bon-' He shook his head at the sight. 'Lookit at them slave scarecrows – walkin' into that bon-bon-bon-bon as if they was paddling.'

'The destruction of evil, Worzel,' said the Crowman quietly.

The scarecrow looked puzzled. 'Disjunction of eelive, eh? 'Ere, Mister Crowman, your all-knowingness – whyfor *is* 'e so eelive?'

The travelling scarecrow-maker swung round on them, his blank face still wearing its sinister smile. 'Why am I so evil? Why am I so evil?' he hissed. 'I'll show you why I'm so evil!' He clawed at his face and tore it off – it had been a mask all along, and behind the mask the horrible truth was exposed; there was nothing more than a crude, half-carved turnip head, with slits for the eyes and mouth, and no nose at all.

Worzel Gummidge gawped. 'Well I'll be bumswizzled! 'E's a scarecrow!'

'Yes,' he spat. 'I am the scarecrow without a name!'

The Crowman's worst fears were confirmed. 'So it *is* you! I

124

always wondered what became of my half-completed scarecrow.'

'The one you *wouldn't* complete, Master,' said the faceless scarecrow bitterly.

The Crowman was unmoved. 'Because it was evil. I felt the evil even as I carved you. And this is how you take your revenge.'

'I live for revenge, my Master!' screamed the faceless scarecrow. He seized an axe and advanced on the Crowman. 'And I shall have it! You may destroy my slaves but you have no power over me!'

'Run, Worzel!' the Crowman cried. 'Run, Aunt Sally! Run for your lives!' and the trio made for the darkness of the woods as fast as their legs could carry them, with the crazed figure of the faceless scarecrow brandishing its axe at their backs.

The travelling scarecrow-maker gave up the chase and watched them go. 'Live another day then, Master. *And* your scarecrow. *And* his doll. But never fear – I have not finished with you yet!' he vowed.

In the calm of his house the Crowman treated Worzel Gummidge and Aunt Sally to a splendid high tea, and explained his terrible mistake as they stuffed themselves with cake. 'It taught me a lesson. Never make a scarecrow from a blighted turnip. I'm convinced that's where the evil came from.'

Aunt Sally belched daintily. 'What *Hi* don't hunderstand, begging your Honour's pardon, is hafter hall what 'e's done to me an' Worzel, why you didn't chuck 'im on the bonfire with the rest of 'em?'

He shook his head sadly. 'As he said, Aunt Sally, I have no power over him. You see, he is the source of the evil that we're fighting. And no matter how much evil we stamp out, we can never quench its source.' Aunt Sally slipped away from the table as the Crowman spoke, and disappeared behind the Japanese lacquer screen.

'Well I's 'ad enough o' fightin' eelive for one day, Mister Crowman sir,' Worzel Gummidge declared with feeling. 'Can I 'ave another bun else do I 'ave to eat some bread an' butter fust?'

The Crowman beamed. 'We can do better than buns, Worzel. Have you forgotten today's your head's birthday?'

'I 'ad forgotten, Mister Crowman, an' tha'ss a fack,' Worzel admitted.

'Time for your birthday cake.' The Crowman pushed back his chair, stood up and beckoned the scarecrow. 'Come along, Worzel. Come along, Aunt ...' He looked round with surprise when he realized that Aunt Sally was no longer there. With a weary expression he pushed aside the screen to reveal her sitting among a litter of cake crumbs and decorations, licking her lips and hiccuping. 'Oh, Aunt Sally!' he reproached her.

'Never mind – I forgives 'er,' said Worzel generously. ''Ere, your magnitude, seein' as 'ow it's my 'ead's birthday an' seein' as 'ow she's scoffed my cake, can I give 'er a kiss?'

The Crowman laughed. 'That's up to Aunt Sally.'

Aunt Sally blushed. 'Well – in the special circumspecstances – just one.'

'Oh, go on then,' said the Crowman.

'Ahem!' coughed Aunt Sally daintily.

'Oh – excuse me!' The Crowman pulled the screen wide again to give them a little privacy, and strolled out, humming softly, to take the air in his cobbled courtyard.